Lord of the High Valley

by

MARGARET WAY

D0188547

Harlequin Books

TORONTO • LONDON • LOS ANGELES • AMSTERDAM
SYDNEY • HAMBURG • PARIS • STOCKHOLM • ATHENS • TOKYO

Original hardcover edition published in 1980
by Mills & Boon Limited

ISBN 0-373-02387-1

Harlequin edition published February 1981

Printed in U.S.A.

Ross was still fast asleep beside her

"I love you," Rosanne whispered soundlessly as she looked with yearning into his face. "I love you. And now you are going to wake up and your eyes will turn to splinters of ice and you'll say things that tear me to pieces."

His skin was so dark, polished bronze. She wanted to touch him, trace the lines of his mouth. He had a scar on his right shoulder, a bad one that had been caused by the rip of a bull's horn.

Rosanne wanted to kiss it, but if she did she would wake him and he would annihilate her with a glance. She hadn't picked this man to love. It had happened, and she was beyond caring.

MARGARET WAY
is also the author of these
Harlequin Romances

and these
Harlequin Presents

CHAPTER ONE

WHEN she opened her eyes, there was a man standing at the window of her room, looking out over the hospital grounds. Even with his back to her, she knew instinctively that he was not a doctor. Doctors exuded a quiet confidence, compassion, not an intimidating aura of challenge.

She saw a tall, commanding figure, ebony head arched high, a handsome, hawkish profile, and deep down inside her, she knew fear. Who *was* he?

She must have made a sound, some strangled little gasp of reaction, for he swung about immediately and looked down at her.

'So you're awake?'

'Yes.' Under the top sheet, her slight breast rose and fell as she tried to contain her panic. 'You're not a doctor, are you?' Doctors didn't wear such ungentle expressions or send convulsive shivers along the spine.

'No,' he returned curtly. 'Not at all.' He spun a chair towards him, settled it nearer the bed and lowered his powerful, hard muscled frame into it. 'The name is McAdam, Miss Grey. Ross McAdam.'

'Oh!' Sweat broke out at her temples and her green eyes were immense and tragic. 'Robin's stepbrother. He ... he ... told me about you.'

'*Did* he?' he stopped her with his hard tone. 'It's only fair to warn you, he told me about you as well.'

'*Warn* me?' Her almond eyes swallowed up her white face. 'Warn me of what?'

'Can you really bear to hear about it?'

'I don't know what you're talking about.' His tone was terrible, cold and cutting, and she made a pathetic little gesture as though to ward him off. 'I'll never forget what has brought tragedy to us all.' Never, *never*, she repeated to herself.

'Remorse, Rosanne?' he challenged her, making her beautiful name sound unpleasant.

'It was an accident, you must know that!' She had to bite hard on her soft mouth to stop the tears of shock.

'Except I haven't come here to discuss that.'

'Then what?' She wished desperately for the strength to leap to her feet and run away. She knew he didn't pity her, would never pity her, no matter what she had been through.

'How could I not come?' he countered harshly. 'You have no one, have you?'

'I have friends.'

'You're bound to have!' His glittery eyes sparkled over her. 'Most of whom are your own age, all of them connected with your own world and none capable of looking after you during your convalesence.'

'God in heaven, *you're* not offering?' She clasped her hands tightly to disguise their trembling. He had an attractive speaking voice, dark and resonant, yet it fell on her ears so gratingly she had difficulty not wincing.

'Robin's mother wants to meet you.' His eyes were frozen lakes of silver and they made him seem even more dangerous. 'You *do* see that she might?'

She looked back at him, saw the hard, unyielding lines of his face and tried to explain. 'I'm sorry...so *sorry* ....'

'Because you couldn't bring yourself to do the correct, natural thing?'

'I don't expect you to understand, but when we first became engaged, I begged Robin to tell his mother, his family.'

'Yet I have a letter from him putting the lie to that.'

'But you *can't*!' she cried, startled.

'I'd show it to you,' he offered curtly, 'only I don't think you could stand any more hurt now.'

'Then what are you trying to do now, if not hurt me?' she accused him. 'It's obvious you dislike me on sight.'

'Do I?' His eyes met hers, coldly brilliant.

'Why won't you believe me?' She hung her pale head. 'It was Robin who wanted it all kept a secret. *Robin*. He even grew angry when I said I would write.'

'So you didn't?'

'No.' She shuddered at his tone. 'At least he was right about something. He told me you would disapprove of me and how important it was you shouldn't.'

'What?' His laugh was brief and humourless. 'Disapprove of a little ballet dancer who happened to net herself a rich young man?'

For a moment Rosanne was silent and her small, naturally pale face went a stark alabaster white. 'How cruel you are!'

'And you are not?' He was looking at her strangely, as though searching her to the soul.

'No.' She put her hand to her mouth shakily, saying, 'No, *no*!'

'Nevertheless, my stepmother desperately wants to look after you, spoil you. In fact, she's tearing herself to pieces about it.'

'I didn't know.' She whispered it penitently, suddenly feeling the other woman's pain.

'You know now.' He was leaning back in the chair, looking straight at her, his silver eyes narrowed.

'So what do you want me to do?'

'Come back with me, my dear, to High Valley.'

'No, I *can't*!' She was aghast at the thought of being trapped into a situation with him, her enemy and a deadly one. 'I'm very grateful, but I can't!'

'Oh, you'll come,' he corrected her softly. 'You owe Marta that much. In a way, you're all she has left of Robin.'

'Did he also write to his mother?' she asked.

'No, only me.' He gave her a hard, contemptuous look. 'He called you a witch, and I can see your green eyes.'

'And yet he loved me.'

'It sounded more like fascination. There hardly seems enough of you to cast a strong spell.'

'Whatever Robin wrote to you,' she said slowly, 'he must have had his reasons, and meeting you now I can understand why he might wish to blame me. He craved your approval all his life and never once did he get it.'

'Go on,' he demanded curtly, 'that's what he told you?'

'What's the use of discussing it?' she whispered tragically. 'Robin's dead, and I wish I'd gone with him.'

'Because you loved him?' His silver eyes never left her face, blazingly alive.

'Why do you think I became engaged to him?' she faltered, giving him an overwhelming advantage.

'You're an orphan, are you not?'

'No family,' she replied, and gave a broken little laugh. 'But there was no mystery surrounding my parentage, Mr McAdam. I'm sure you've raked that much up.'

'Shall we say I know as much about you as I need to know.'

Rosanne swallowed and brushed a shaky hand across her forehead. 'You sound so grim, you must be blaming me for everything, yet it was an *accident*. The other car simply came from nowhere!'

'And Robin failed to stop at a STOP sign. An established fact.' The dark face was showing its own strain. 'You were sitting beside him, Miss Grey. Both of you must have been deeply engrossed. In what, an argument?'

'You would naturally think that.' She struggled painfully against her tears. 'It was very late and Robin was sometimes a little reckless at the wheel.'

'Then you must have been out of your mind to go with him!'

'*Please!*' She put both hands over her ears, shocked and trembling, and the colour ran under the dark polished texture of his skin.

'Forgive me!' He bent his jet-black head. 'The news was an appalling shock. My stepmother will never recover from it. She adored her son, though she fretted endlessly about the way he lived his life.'

'As *you* did?'

'One can't condone waste, Miss Grey.'

Rosanne felt the dead weight of his condemnation on her slight shoulders. 'You're so brutally uncompromising!'

'I might seem so to a child, but the truth is often unbearable. Whatever you feel about me is entirely unimportant. It's my stepmother who has to be considered now.'

'She may not like me at all.'

'She'll like the look of you,' he said flatly, 'and I'm

sure you can manage the rest. Acting ability must be a priceless asset to a dancer.'

'I won't come. It can't be wise.' She looked away over his head, wanting to weep.

'I've spoken to your doctor. It will be six to eight weeks before you're ready to take up your exhausting life again. In the meantime, you'll offer comfort where it's needed.'

'And that's what it's all about.'

'It's about *you* as well!' he bit off harshly. 'You look as though the breeze would blow you away.'

'I must think about it.' She was panicked by the sound of her own shaky voice, defeated.

'Say yes and save my time.' Ross McAdam looked and spoke like a man who was never thwarted. 'Quite frankly I can't see what else you *can* do.'

'Yet you regard me as an enemy. For whatever reason, you've decided to hate me.'

'My dear child,' he said coldly, 'hate is a very big word.'

'But you won't deny it.'

'Oh, for God's sake!' he swung up and half turned away from her. 'You were Robin's fiancée. You obviously need caring for and neither myself nor my stepmother can possibly shut our eyes to the situation. Had Robin lived, you might have become family. As things stand, I have to tell you he made no provision for you in his will. The McAdam money reverts to High Valley.'

'To *you*!' she countered with uncharacteristic bitterness.

'I'm sure Robin told you all about it.' His black brows formed a V and he looked powerful and dangerous with a potential for violence.

'He told me very little about his home,' she said.

'But as he never worked, I'm sure you realised he

was a very rich young man.'

'So?' There was a flash of anger in her soft voice and a gathering storm in her eyes. 'Why should you mention money? I never exploited him.'

'I'm sure your engagement ring is as big and green as your eyes. Don't cry,' he added suavely, with no real concern.

'Why should I?' The crying would come later. 'I've done nothing with which to reproach myself. Robin gave me something much more important than expensive gifts. He gave me confidence and security. He was so warm and friendly and so much fun. I never had much fun in my life. The aunt who reared me after my parents were killed wasn't a very tolerant woman.'

'Yet she encouraged your talent?' Sunlight struck the strong bones of his face, an arresting face, though the very sight of him made her heart sink.

'In the beginning, it was somewhere to send me on Saturday mornings,' she explained. 'Later on, she did take some pride in me. It suited her temperament to have her niece achieve some small fame and repay the fees.' She didn't mention all the lessons her wonderful teacher had given her for nothing.

'And Robin?' he prompted with deceptive gentleness, 'he loved your dancing?'

'He thought it perfection.' Her green eyes went dreamy, remembering.

'A dark spell!' His face tightened and a betraying anger showed in his eyes. 'Apparently he wasn't the only one.'

'To like my dancing?' A flush sprang to her delicate high cheekbones.

'To fall under your spell.'

'All right, so he wrote to you about André. It was

a mistake. I'd hurt myself and André was only trying to comfort me.'

'I don't think you believe that, any more than Robin did.'

'I never realised he was so jealous!' she whispered.

'Then you would have been more discreet?'

'Think what you like of me, but you're quite wrong. My talents are only for the dance.'

He stared at her, his silver eyes kindling in his dark face. 'You forget, little one, I know all about you.'

'And *Robin* told you?' She looked back at him, stunned.

'Many things, and you match the picture.'

'Then I don't undestand!' Her slight body seemed to crumble.

'What are you, anyway? Eighteen, nineteen? Only able to function in a world of makebelieve.'

'Perhaps you're right!' She felt her vision waver. 'As you know so much about me, you know I was orphaned as a small child. Without a penny, a home, or the parents who loved me. I've never really known what it's like to be self-assured and secure.'

'Except on the stage.'

'I belong there,' she said simply.

'Yet you prayed for a good husband?' The arrogant mouth curled derisively.

'No. Robin wanted me.' Rosanne spoke the simple truth.

Again that cruelly sardonic look. 'You did nothing to attract him, of course. Yet your closest friend told me you two had a little contest going.'

He might just as well have struck her, she was so shocked. '*My* closest friend?' she echoed.

'Sorry—girl friends would be too competitive to get really close.'

'I think someone was having a game with you.'

'I'm not easily taken in,' he said sharply, his eyes like diamonds against his dark skin. 'At least a half a dozen members of your own company spoke of your capacity for generating much feeling, both in your dancing and ... elsewhere. I imagine it adds a touch of excitement. Or spice.'

She turned her blonde head away with an effort. 'Hurt me,' she muttered. 'You seem to enjoy it.'

'I'm not trying to hurt you,' he said forcibly, 'but there's a price to be paid for everything.'

'And you don't take retribution lightly.' She sighed and when she looked up again, he was studying her so cynically, she knew instant dread.

'You didn't love him, did you?' he asked.

'How can you say that?' Her green eyes looked frightened. Of course she hadn't. Not with the desperate passion she read about in books and scarcely thought could happen to her. Security was more important; to feel loved and wanted. Such was the drawback of being young and totally alone in the world.

'But I can!' he returned bitingly. 'Robin confided in me.'

'He confided nothing. . . .' she began, and faltered, thinking of the occasional strange mood that so changed Robin's colourful and gay personality. That was something which had appealed to her from the very first; that, and his dark, laughing eyes. So different from his stepbrother's, so shockingly different.

'I see you remember?' He gave an explosive, impatient sigh.

'You can't believe me, because you don't really *want* to!' she said urgently. 'I'm not sure what Robin told you, but I never betrayed him. He thought——'

'Like everyone else did——'

'*No!*' She put her pretty, slender hands to her

temples as though to block out her thoughts. 'Robin was always so sweet to me, but he was a little paranoid about being overshadowed. I didn't realise it until. . . .'

'André?' he supplied brutally.

'André is my friend. No more.'

'And you found you couldn't handle it? A girl like you who likes to play games.'

'Then why do you want me?' She swept up her silver-gilt head, too deep in panic to try to defend herself.

'I told you,' he looked down at her broodingly. 'You and only you hold the key to my stepmother's recovery. She has strong need of you and I've done nothing, said nothing to blacken your character.'

'And I'm perfectly sure you will, the minute Robin's mother is well.'

'Of course.' He bowed suavely and for a minute he reminded her of the Devil, lean and dark and satanically handsome.

'You shock me,' she told him.

'I understand very well how you feel.'

'Do you?' She gave a ragged little laugh. 'Plots happen all the time, deliberate plots. Obviously someone wants to discredit me and you don't much care to check the story out.'

'The tragedy is, I can't check it out with Robin!' Ross McAdam turned away deliberately and looked out of the window, the set of his head and his wide shoulders conveying his inevitable antagonism. 'Why should Robin of all people turn treacherous, when he loved you?'

'I don't know!' Rosanne cried out her bewilderment. 'Maybe I didn't know him at all—who he was, what he was. I'm nineteen. Maybe I haven't learned anything except how to express myself dancing.

Ballet has been everything to me as I had nothing else
to love.'

'Yet apparently you had plenty of admirers?' He
still stood at the huge window with his back to her.

'One does when one dances well.'

'Even I can appreciate that!' He turned around
and flashed a glance at her. 'You're tired.'

'Yes. I'll feel much better when you've gone.'

He bowed slightly again, and a thin smile curved
over a chiselled mouth. 'You and I had better make a
treaty right now. In front of Marta we're friends and
you'll live better than you ever dreamed of.'

'For how long?' she asked.

'Months.'

'I can't bear to think about it.'

'If you do your part,' he said coolly, 'and help
Marta, I'll send you back to your own little world
with a clear profit.'

'You *beast*!' She pulled the pillow from the back
of her head and threw it at him. 'I didn't know anyone could be so rotten!'

'You're damned right they can!' He crossed to her
bedside, put a steely hand to her back and rearranged
the pillow. 'I care for my stepmother a great deal and
whether you want it or not, you're going to come with
me and give no trouble.'

'And if I don't?' She felt seared to the skin by the
touch of his hand.

'Do you think you can deal with all the hospital
bills?' he asked ironically. 'This is a private room
and you've had the very best of attention.'

'Oh God!' Rosanne lay back looking fragile and
exhausted. Curse her own stupidity! Why hadn't she
guessed at the room to herself instead of a ward?
The amazing thing was, she hadn't, thinking they
were keeping her quiet. Pain and deep shock had

made her numb and uncaring. Now harsh reality had set in. There was very little between her and starvation if she couldn't work. Nevertheless she said proudly: 'I'll find some way to pay you back.'

'But not right away.' His insolence took her breath away and the shining, frozen eyes ran disparagingly over her slight figure beneath the bedclothes. 'I don't imagine ballet dancers earn very much money until they're famous.'

Rosanne said nothing, hating the predatory smile on his handsome mouth.

Let him think what he liked of her. An unlikely femme fatale luring men to destruction. A promiscuous little dancer. A liar. A cheat, devious and designing. He was a stranger, cold and dangerous, and she was innocent of his every charge. Robin had meant more to her than any other young man she had ever known. Yet Robin had ultimately betrayed her. For his own sake. Whether he had really thought her involved with André, it still didn't explain the harmful way he had written of her to his stepbrother.

She would have to think hard about Robin—how he had turned on her without warning, reproaching her wildly with his imaginings. She had thought she had convinced him and they had been happy enough that last night. Poor Robin, filled with a heavy desire to be first. He, too, had gone in awe of the lord of the High Valley. The title sprang instantly to her mind, consistent with her vivid impressions and just as menacing.

'What are you thinking?' Ross McAdam came to the head of the bed and looked down at her gravely.

'Oh, how terrible it is to want vengeance!' Her great almond eyes searched his face.

'You're very fanciful,' he drawled.

'It fits you, that image.'

'No matter. The only thing that really matters is that you help Marta. She's waiting for you with open arms. Keep that firmly in your mind.'

Rosanne shrugged, a tiny graceful motion of her shoulders, and his mouth tightened. 'I think that's all we have to say to one another. I'm returning to High Valley at the end of the week, by which time you'll have your dismissal from hospital.'

'And what about clothes? I'd have to go home and pack.'

The silvery eyes didn't waver. 'I think I can arrange all you need.'

'Please allow me to say you *can't*!' She found her voice compulsively. 'My clothes may be very inadequate by your standards, but they'll do.'

'As you like!' His strange eyes explored her face deeply. 'Until Saturday, then, Miss Grey.'

A soft shiver ran through her and she moved back against the pillows. 'It must be easy for a man of power to crush people.'

'Ah then, I've the feeling for all your fragility, you have some steel in you. I've never taken much of an interest in ballet, but I'm told you're very good.'

'Perhaps you'll come and see me dance some day,' she said defiantly.

'I think not.' His white teeth flashed in a smile without humour. 'I'm a very busy man, quite without sensitivity.'

'That I know.' For an instant her green eyes blazed and the colour ran in to her small triangular face. There was a lump of anger in her throat. Anger, excitement, and she could have screamed aloud at his arrogant oppressiveness, only someone came to the door—a visitor. And as they turned their heads together, a slim young man of middle height launched himself into the room, his sparkling black eyes flicking from one to the other.

'Excuse me—I'm not intruding?'

Rosanne was struck dumb, but Ross McAdam said briefly: 'I'm just leaving.'

'How are you, *mignonne*?' André turned to Rosanne tenderly, his charmingly accented voice as gentle as his quick smile. Rosanne was his great favourite, both as a partner and a young girl, but there had never been anything between them, to André's amused consternation. Amused, before a young Greek god called Robin.

'Won't you introduce us?' Ross McAdam admonished her, brilliant intelligence in his light eyes.

'The little one isn't usually so slow!' André turned his glossy head in the older man's direction, his winning smile on his mobile face. 'André LeStrange, sir, and you?'

'Ross McAdam.'

André had put out his hand automatically, but he paled. 'Robin's brother?'

'Stepbrother.' Ross McAdam looked down his nose and his eyes glittered with an odd expression. 'You didn't like him.'

'No, I didn't like him,' André said soberly. 'But I was very sorry to hear of his tragic death. This is true. As for Rosanne, she could have been killed.'

'But she wasn't. A great mercy.'

Ross's tone almost unnerved André, who turned to look at Rosanne. 'We're all determined to look after her. And why not? Don't we all love her?'

'As a sister?' Ross McAdam smiled at him and André coloured under his sallow skin, misliking that chill smile.

'We in the ballet have a duty towards one another.'

'Just as we have to Robin's fianceé.' Ross McAdam looked down at him from his much superior height.

'Rosanne no doubt will be telling you how she's coming back with me to High Valley. My stepmother has insisted she spend her convalescence with us.'

'Yes, of course,' André murmured at last. It was never good to cross a man who had the radiance of the devil.

Afterwards when he had gone, André gazed at Rosanne despairingly. 'How did you ever consent, *chérie*?'

'I owe it to Robin's mother. I've never met her,' Rosanne said in a low voice.

'I'm afraid of that man!' André lifted his black eyes to the ceiling. 'Yet why should *I* be afraid?'

'I think he has that effect on everyone.'

'You, too?' A shadow crossed André's expressive face. 'He must be what's called a despot. A *grand seigneur* in the old days.'

'Feudal, yes.' Rosanne sighed and shook her head. 'How strange you should call at that very minute.'

'Does it matter?' André came forward and took her two hands. He was a young man of deep, passing emotions and Rosanne had fascinated him for some time.

'I think Robin mentioned your name,' she told him.

'God!' André was disturbed and greatly startled. 'So that's why he looked at me so strangely. The intensity of his eyes. He would be a man of fierce loyalty.'

'He is.' She didn't say there was a frightening resentment in him against her. More a kind of hatred.

'One would never have taken them for brothers, even stepbrothers, half brothers, actually,' mused André. 'There is no point of resemblance.'

A nurse entered the room silently and both of them started.

'Time for your medication, dear!' the nurse smiled at Rosanne.

'Shall I go?' André looked into the nurse's plain, pleasant face and her colour rose.

'Not at all!' She was a little confused at seeing one of her favourite male dancers in person, but he hardly noticed her. 'Just two little pills.' She gave Rosanne her kind, comforting smile and put the capsules into Rosanne's outstretched hand.

'Thank you.'

'You're looking a little pale. Feel all right?'

'Fine.' Rosanne returned the smile and swallowed the capsules down.

'Very well, dear,' the nurse answered, thinking everything the girl in the bed did was incredibly graceful—the turn of her wrist and that swan-like neck. Not beautiful really, except on stage, but haunting, a little fey.

André was waiting for her to go, so the nurse pressed Rosanne's hand. 'If you need anything, dear, just press the call button.'

'You're very good to me.' Rosanne gave the quick, eloquent smile that so illuminated her pale features.

'And you're a fine one to spoil.' The nurse crossed the floor and went out of the room.

'Do you think this is what they're going to do? Spoil you?' André asked uncertainly.

'The McAdams?' Rosanne picked up the water glass again. Her throat was so dry.

'There's more to this than meets the eye!' André's long dark hair was rising in a crest. He was dressed very casually in a T-shirt and tight jeans and he looked attractive, faintly scruffy, with an overt sexuality. 'Now that I think of it, McAdam asked to meet some members of the company. It was days ago when

I was doing a guest spot. Why should he want to do that?'

'Merely to meet some of my friends.' Rosanne looked at him with her beautiful, sad eyes.

'Nothing as simple as that! If he spoke to Danielle, she would be damnable. You know her cruel tongue, and she hates you for your beautiful, balanced harmony, the magic you bring to your roles.' André paced to the window, then turned to look back at her. 'Danielle would cause trouble if she could. Her every word is laden with insinuation and she's impossibly jealous of you.'

'What could she say?' Rosanne felt colder now. Danielle was a very capable dancer, physically striking too, but no one in the company liked her and all the girls feared her poisoned tongue.

'She could say you and I were having a passionate love affair behind your fiancé's back. Or you set out to fascinate every male in the company, one by one. I've heard her say that. Of course it's not true. You don't know your own gifts.'

'Why should she want to harm me?' For a terrible moment Rosanne saw how it might have been.

'Jealousy, *petite*. It's an acid.'

At his words something clicked inside Rosanne's head. Danielle was capable of treachery. Look how she had made mischief between Lisa and Ray, hoping to drive them apart. Now André had confirmed that Ross McAdam had had conversation with different members of the company. He had told her himself of her mysterious 'girl friend' who had fed him such lies.

No wonder he thought her so cheap and conniving! Danielle got her kicks out of creating chaos and she had positively loathed Rosanne since the Director had promoted her over the heads of the whole corps.

'So how long are you going to be away from us?' André stood facing her, digging deeply into the pockets of his blue jeans. 'A dancer can't afford to lose time. Not to work—a *disaster*!'

'I *need* time, André!' Rosanne's great eyes looked tormented. 'Robin is dead and I could have been killed.'

'Darling!' André gathered her up in concern. 'You mustn't torture yourself about Robin. He might have represented love to you, security, all the things you've never known, but he was altogether a strange person. He never worked. I mean, who does not work? He wouldn't want to share you, do you know that? In time I'm sure he would have torn you away from the dance. You saw how he reacted when he found you in my arms, so innocently, like now, offering comfort. He was a deep one. Maybe it's better not to think how he was. God rest his soul! But he would have made you very unhappy. Such a person has problems, and having met his brother I can see why he defected from this cattle kingdom, how is it High Valley. What would my little Rose be doing there?' With his head bent over her, her fragile body half in his arms, André surrendered to in irresistible impulse and kissed the side of her mouth. Her small, tilted breasts were thrust against the soft fabric of her nightgown and he was afraid at the extent of his own desire. Marriage was bondage, a terrible bondage, but he badly wanted to make love to this medieval little nun, had wanted to for a long time.

'Rosanne?' He could feel her unresponsiveness, yet it drew him on. No one who could dance with such beauty and passion could remain a virgin for ever. He knew that her fiancé had wanted her urgently, just as he knew Rosanne had accepted her fiancé because he had been the first person outside of their own world who had ever been kind to her. She knew nothing of love.

Rosanne was silent, but the tears were running over her pale cheeks. Lost in her own thoughts, the terrible shock of meeting Ross McAdam, she felt nothing of André's desire. He was her friend who only sought to console her. She threw her head back against his arm and in that moment André lowered his head. No more waiting!

'*Excuse me.*'

A voice sounded across the room so coldly, so warningly, André jumped to his feet and spun to face the man at the door like a wary adversary. 'You've come back!'

'So I have.'

'What for, to find me out?' André's voice was rising slightly and his gamin face was showing its anxiety. Bones could be broken so easily and if McAdam was going to throw him out he would have no chance.

'I don't think I need worry about you at all,' Ross McAdam said flatly. 'All the same, you can get out.'

'André, please stay!' Rosanne begged like a desolate child, but André had no intention of staying where he was. Survival was important.

'It's terribly necessary you don't blame Rosanne,' he said bravely. 'You must see she was only looking for comfort.'

'Supposing you go.' Ross McAdam walked towards him and André pulled nervously at the neck of his green T-shirt.

'*All right!* Don't blame me too much. The little one attracts men like moths!'

'Oh, André!' Rosanne put her hands to her wet cheeks and rubbed them in agitation. She had found that remark unpardonable and from the ominous expression on Ross McAdam's dark face André's departure would have to be imminent. How could a man's eyes be so frightening? He must have come back just to check on them. Oh, damn him! *Damn* him!

André leapt to the door like a puppet on a string and belatedly waved to Rosanne. 'Sorry, darling, but I'm not awfully brave!'

She had to acknowledge that, and her small heart-shaped face was alive with colour. 'Goodbye, André.' He too had betrayed her.

'Mr McAdam. . . .' André said, and gave a vague kind of salute before he disappeared.

'You really are a puzzle, do you know that?' Ross McAdam was staring at her, his silver eyes stark and brilliant. 'You look as if not a shadow of passion has touched you in your life, yet you have a reputation for provocative behaviour.'

'Who told you?' Against the sudden flush in her cheeks, her eyes glowed like emeralds. 'Someone called Danielle?'

'I've seen you with my own eyes.'

'How proud of yourself you must be. To be a spy!'

'I frankly admit it,' he said curtly. 'After all, what's wrong with checking on you? You yourself asked me to do it.'

It was useless to try and defend herself. He had diminished her in every way. 'I want to be alone, Mr McAdam. Will you please go away.'

'I didn't want to leave without telling you I've just spoken to Sister and you may be discharged a day earlier. Dr Haarman will verify that and I'll be in touch with him.'

'You're so good at making me pay,' she said bitterly.

'Don't we all pay for our sins?'

Rosanne couldn't answer him but continued to stare woodenly at the door long after he had gone. He terrified her—a hard man, entirely without pity. Her only hope was Robin's mother. What would she be like? Very kind to want a girl who had never found the courage to disobey Robin and write to his mother. Yet how could she avoid confrontations with the man who despised her? She needed to get well and quickly, not walk into a steel trap.

For the rest of the day she sank into a sad, unreachable mood and no matter how hard Dr Haarman tried to cheer her with his good news the only reality was the thought that soon she would be living at High Valley.

CHAPTER TWO

ROSANNE was nervous in the plane and slightly sick, and when Ross told her he was making a stop-over midway between the capital and his property, she could have sighed aloud with relief. She had never in her life flown in a light aircraft, and now notwithstanding the fact that it was a big, pressurised eightseater, she couldn't wait to get out. The cockpit, the isolation, the dangerous man beside her, all contributed towards her trembling claustrophobia.

'You're not sick, are you?' he demanded.

'A little.' They were the first words he had addressed to her in more than twenty minutes.

'We'll be putting down shortly.'

'Safely, I hope.'

'Why don't you shut your eyes,' he said mockingly, 'instead of sitting there like a terrified child.'

'Not that bad, surely?'

'Oh, my God!' He turned to glance at her and his mouth quirked.

'Are these friends of yours?' she asked politely in her soft, gentle voice.

'You wonder I have any?'

'You couldn't possibly treat everyone the way you treat me.'

'Really?' he looked at her in faint surprise. 'I thought I was treating you pretty well, and the fact you haven't said thank you hasn't escaped me.'

'I told you I'd find some way to pay you back.'

'Where's the emerald?' he asked abruptly. Just like that.

'My ring?'

'Yes.' This time his tone was clipped to something like anger. 'You don't wear it.'

'It's round my neck.' With a little difficulty, because her fingers were trembling, Rosanne withdrew the gold chain, the magnificent emerald warm where it had lain between her breasts.

'I guess you don't know where it came from?' He gave her a lancing look.

'A jeweller. A good one.' The light caught the diamonds that encircled the beautiful deep green stone like petals.

'Give it to me.' He held out his left hand.

'Right now?'

'Before we put down. You can't wear it. The ring belonged to my mother.'

'But Robin gave it to me!' Would she always be shocked in his presence?

'So he did. Without anyone's knowledge.'

'I don't *believe* it!' She almost flung the stone into his hand and he put it away in his breast pocket.

'My dear, I don't think you knew too much about Robin.'

Rosanne swallowed hard and the burning colour flooded her cheeks, giving her face a strange beauty. 'I can only remember how kind he was to me. All the fun and the flowers.'

'Not the bad spells?'

'There weren't any.' The sky was a glorious, dense blue and she felt badly about lying.

'You're not going to admit to them?'

'Not to you.' She glanced down at the sea of plain, the sun-baked earth. They were descending and she could see flocks of sheep, ridiculously small against the giant landscape. 'It's so big!' she exclaimed.

'Bigger than a stage.'

'That's understood.' She sighed a little at his unrelenting attitude. 'What shall I say about not wearing Robin's ring?'

'You needn't be afraid—I've taken care of it. It's a diamond, a big one. You'll love it.'

'Please don't!' she begged.

'You don't like diamonds?' He glanced at her with a narrow smile.

'I prefer flowers.'

'You'd look a little ridiculous with one tied around your finger.' He could see the pulse beating in the hollow of her throat. 'I'd like you to forget Robin ever gave you that emerald. Or that you've ever seen it.'

'Are you trying to tell me Robin stole it? I couldn't bear that.'

'Probably he was fascinated by your green eyes.'

They were passing over some outbuildings now

and Rosanne could see the landing strip coming up. 'Please help me!' She didn't know why she cried it except that she was so utterly confused.

'You need it.' Surprisingly Ross's voice held a touch of pity. 'The people you're going to meet are the Grant-Taylors. I've known them all my life. Clive was a good friend of my father's and his wife, Sarina, was my mother's bridesmaid. Their son and heir, Philip, was killed in a riding accident three years ago. Now only Francine is left.'

'And they all knew Robin?'

'But of course.'

'Then I'm going to need a lot of courage.' She twisted her hands together because they were trembling.

'Not nearly as much as when you land on High Valley.'

Preoccupied with the familiar rite of bringing the plane in, Ross took no further notice of her, so he didn't see her shut her eyes. Her heart was pounding and there were painful cramps in her stomach. She should relax. He had made her wear her seat-belt all along and now it seemed to be cutting into her shoulder.

They were dropping rapidly, yet the touchdown when it came was so smooth that involuntarily she relaxed all her bones.

'You'll have to get used to light aircraft if you're going to remain any time with us,' said Ross.

'I'm not a good traveller at any time,' she said vaguely. They were taxiing along the strip towards the silver glinting hangar and what appeared to be a boundary fence. There was no one in sight, but off to the left she could see a rising swirl of dust.

'Is there no one to meet us?' Ross had shut down the twin engines and in the sudden silence her voice sounded very young and frightened.

'Francine is bound to have spotted the plane.' He unbuckled his seat-belt and because she looked so helpless leant over and released her as well. 'Come on, snap out of it!'

He started to move, going back to the rear door, and Rosanne followed, her legs trembling beneath her. He had stopped a few paces away, waiting for her to catch up, and when she did he picked up her left hand and held it.

'Sorry it's not as good as last time. But good enough!'

His voice cut into her and her hand burned, but still he held it, pushing home on her slender finger a beautiful and expensive solitaire diamond.

'How I *hate* you!' She flushed scarlet and tried to jerk away.

'After all I've done for you?' He gave her a brilliant, ironical stare.

'I'm not sure I can handle this.' Her heart was beating so hard she was suffocating.

'What kind of talk is that? You look so damned vulnerable, but I know better.' A little violently he opened out the door and dropped the steps into place. 'What did you used to say to yourself when you were a little girl? I can do anything I really want to.'

He was down on the ground before her, looking up, a handsome man of a powerful and compelling personality.

From being overheated, she was suddenly ice cold. She heard him say her name and she rubbed a hand over her face then looked back at him. Sunlight illuminated his tall frame, but his dark face was in shadow. Up in the sky, a single eagle was cruising. It was all so terribly unfamiliar; a blazingly hot solitude, empty of sound. Rosanne drooped her blonde head and gave an anguished, unaware little cry, then she fell straight out of the plane into his powerful, extended arms....

When she returned to full consciousness, she was lying a few hundred yards away in the ribbon shade of a tree. Ross McAdam was supporting her and a young woman was staring at her with snapping hazel eyes. 'Just take it quietly,' she said, 'you passed out.'

Rosanne glanced upwards at black drawn brows, narrowed silver eyes. He might have expected it from some poor little fool.

'Why don't we get her up to the house?' the young woman was standing up purposefully, dusting off her straight cotton trousers. 'She certainly doesn't look as if she's fit to travel.'

'I'm all right.' Rosanne's fingers gripped Ross McAdam's arms.

'*Are* you?' he looked down at her formidably.

'I don't think I've fainted before in my life.'

'Some people just can't take to flying!' Hazel eyes stood erect, alert and confident.

'Not straight out of hospital,' Ross amended a little shortly. Unconsciously, with his thumb, he was stroking the small hand he held, but his expression suggested nothing gentle. 'I really should have brought you back on a commercial flight.'

'Oh, don't be silly, Ross!' Francine Grant-Taylor looked down at him. 'What are you blaming yourself for?'

'Just look at her.'

'Yes, she is a little waif!' Francine dropped to his side again, the picture of health; tall and glossy with a gleaming, tanned skin. 'When you're ready to move, dear, we'll go up to the house. Take your time.'

'You must be Francine?' Rosanne looked into her eyes gravely.

'Sorry'—Francine gave a little laugh—'you rather put us off the introductions.'

'I'm sorry for that.'

'At any rate, you're here now, and you're only a child!'

'If you're ready Rosanne, I'll lift you,' Ross said as though he hadn't been listening to a word either of the girls had said.

'I think I'd better walk.'

'It's obvious you can't!' His arms tighter round her and all at once he lifted her, a featherweight, with her long blonde hair falling out of its casual knot to spill over his shoulder. She was so dizzy she had to cling to him, and to her amazement he said very gently:

'You'll be better when you've had a rest.'

'She looks better already!' From Francine's expression one would have thought her both surprised and affronted to see a cascade of silky, silver-gilt hair. She stood there in the shadow of the beautiful shade tree, a little stupefied by the turn of events. 'Well, come along now. We can ring though to High Valley and tell them to expect you tomorrow.'

'If you just give me an hour or so, I'll be ready to go on.'

'Better for you to stay. Poor little thing!' Francine led the way, a trim attractive figure with her short, springy brown curls, a glossy bronze in the sun.

They put her into the back of the station wagon and instead of taking the wheel, Francine slid into the passenger side of the front seat. 'I didn't know Robin's fiancée would be as dainty and delicate as a little piece of porcelain.'

Though she spoke smilingly to Rosanne's sensitive ears it sounded as though Francine turned away from fragility. Also she spoke as though Rosanne wasn't there or was too young to understand.

Ross McAdam seemed to have retreated from both of them, putting the car into reverse and then heading off along a wide, beaten track.

'How did it all go?' Francine dropped her voice to a confidential pitch.

'Better than expected. I've bought a new helicopter.'

'I thought the Brahmans were getting too smart for that?'

'They learn fast all right, but we can't do without the aerial mustering.' His light, brilliant eyes fixed themselves on the rear vision. 'How do you feel now, Rosanne?'

'Much better.' She lifted a hand and tried to smooth her hair into some order, but the clasp was gone.

'It must be terrible to be ill.' Francine looked back at her and frowned. The girl looked very delicate and frail and Francine could hardly believe Robin had been interested in her. It was no secret to anyone the way Robin McAdam had lived; selfish, self-centred, self-indulgent with a marked preference for pleasure-seeking sophisticates. Not this child.

'I've spoken to Rosanne's doctor,' Ross said coolly, 'she's a lot stronger than she looks.'

'I imagine dancers would have to be!' Francine waved a hand indulgently. 'Believe me, dear, we all want to care for you. You've been through a great deal.'

Rosanne compressed her soft mouth. Was that what she wanted? To be cared for? She glanced up and met an inimical silver regard.

'If you look up now, Rosanne, you'll see the house,' Francine announced in a proud voice. 'It's not High Valley, but most people are impressed.'

Obediently Rosanne looked out of the window. It was a warm, dry day of great radiance and up ahead, surrounded by acres of gardens and stately shade trees, was a large rambling single-storied building of white-painted timber with the spacious verandahs one associated with Queensland.

'It looks beautiful!' she said,

'We think so.' Francine's smile said plainer than any words, *All this will be coming to me.* 'Of course it hasn't a history like High Valley, but it's a fine example of a colonial mansion house. The property originally belonged to a Colonel Macpherson, one of our earliest settlers—India and all that, decorated for distinguished service. We have a picture of the old boy at the house. I expect you don't know the Outback at all?'

'No.' Rosanne's lashed swept downwards, not ash-gold like her hair, but dark like her delicate, well marked brows. Despite the beauty of her surroundings she felt an immense desire to be back in the little apartment she shared with two of the other girls. Francine, though clad casually, was the picture of country elegance and her own appearance troubled her. She knew she looked about sixteen and an insignificant sixteen at that.

'Oh, it's lovely to have you here, Ross!' Francine said under her breath. Her expression when she looked at Rosanne was patronising and faintly pitying, but when her hazel eyes leapt to Ross McAdam's dark face, they shone with a fierce delight. 'Won't you come riding with me this afternoon. Make me happy?'

'You're forgetting I have to get back to High Valley.'

'Oh, damn High Valley!' She put out a brown hand and just touched his cheek. 'Don't you ever think of anything but work?'

'Well, I might have a swim with you to cool off.'
He glanced at Francine briefly and Rosanne could
hardly credit the change in him. He looked relaxed
and smiling and immensely attractive.

'I *adore* you!' said Francine, apparently forgetting
there was anyone in the whole world but him.

'Why the sigh, little one?' Ross McAdam demanded, very suddenly.

'Was I sighing?' She was perplexed by his unpre-
dictability.

'You were.'

'Take pity on the child!' Francine ran her fingers
through her short dark hair. 'She couldn't possibly
expect to take everything in so soon.'

Everything? That you worship him? Rosanne retired back into herself. They were sweeping up the
drive now, the old circular carriageway, and a man
and woman stationed up on the verandah began to
wave, then came on down the short flight of stairs to
greet them.

The man was silver-haired, elderly, debonair, the
woman very youthful-looking and dressed like her
daughter in straight, slim trousers and a loose-fitting
silk shirt.

'Ross dear!' Mrs Grant-Taylor came forward with
a little rush, looked briefly at Rosanne and smiled,
then stood on tiptoe to kiss Ross McAdam's darkly
tanned cheek.

'Sarina!' He put his arm lightly around her and
shook hands with Francine's father like the good
friends they were.

'Good to see you, my boy. And this is Rosanne.'

'Poor little thing just passed out on us,' Francine
informed both her parents with a wry little grimace.

'Good heavens, you *do* look rather pale!' Sarina

Grant-Taylor frowned in consternation. 'Welcome to Malawarra, my dear. I only wish we could have met under happier circumstances. Robin's death was a great shock to us all.'

'Let's go in out of the sun, shall we?' her husband said smoothy. 'I'm sure Rosanne will feel all the better for a nice cup of tea.'

'Surely you're not continuing on to High Valley, Ross?' Sarina glanced up at the tall man beside her.

'I've been away a long time.'

'But, dear, it's not often we get the chance to see you. Please stay overnight. I'm sure Rosanne will benefit from a good night's sleep.'

'So you're a dancer?' Gently Clive drew Rosanne ahead. 'I should say a good one.'

'Thank you.' Rosanne turned to smile into his kind eyes. 'You have a beautiful property, Mr Grant-Taylor. I should love to be able to walk all round it.'

'And so you shall. Well, perhaps not *walk* and perhaps not today, but certainly some time in the near future. Marta is so looking forward to having you and I know you're going to ease her poor heart.'

'I'm afraid I may disappoint her,' Rosanne said quickly.

'Dear heaven, no!' Clive looked down sideways at her troubled little face. 'After all, Robin loved you, and if I might say so, you're extremely charming.'

'Thank you. I need confidence so much.' Her glittery little smile was full of gratitude. 'You knew Robin well?'

'From the day he was born!' He sighed deeply. 'Our families have always been close. I had a son too, you know.'

'I'm deeply sorry.'

'Ross told you?' They paused on the polished timber verandah, spontaneously relaxed in each other's company.

'Yes.' Rosanne moved her hand in a compassionate little gesture, briefly touching his arm. 'It must take great courage to go on.'

'You know how it is.' A pause ensued, while they both turned to look out over the beautiful gardens. 'Philip had such promise. He was a wonderful son!'

'I'm sure of it,' Rosanne heard herself saying quietly.

'Don't look so sad, dear,' he begged.

'I feel like weeping.'

'Please—I didn't mean to make you more unhappy. You're young, my dear, very young. In time you'll recover and be happy again.'

'If you believe that, so must I.' Rosanne smiled into the kind eyes that looked straight into her own. Down in the brilliant sunshine the others were carrying on an amicable little argument with Francine reaching out her two hands to grasp Ross McAdam's strong arms. Rosanne had no need to guess at what the gesture meant. Francine was determined to delay him. And so was her mother.

'What do you think of Ross?' Clive Grant-Taylor asked her.

'I'm not sure. I think I'm afraid of him.'

'Really?' he gave an understanding little laugh. 'Haven't met anyone like him before?'

'Never.' Rosanne sighed betrayingly. 'He must have been affected painfully by Robin's death.'

'It was a great shock!' This very guardedly. 'At least you were spared, thank God. None of us can pretend Robin didn't like to live dangerously. I'm assuming you were aware of that, my dear. It explains a great deal. Marta, his mother, used to worry a good deal about him. But of course you knew that.'

'He didn't enjoy being away from her ... his family,' Rosanne offered loyally.

'Did he tell you that?'

'Certainly.' Rosanne stared at him. She could hardly have said Robin had told her his stepbrother had done everything in his power to make life at High Valley intolerable for him. 'You look surprised?'

'No, dear. Nothing surprises me any more. Except, perhaps a little, *you*.'

'Please tell me ...' she invited.

'I suppose you're not what we expected.'

At this moment his wife ascended the stairs like a girl, smiling brilliantly. 'Please forgive us, Rosanne, but we had to make certain Ross wasn't going to spirit you away.'

'So we're staying?'

'Indeed you are. Until tomorrow. We all so enjoy Ross's company and now we have the opportunity to get to know you.'

'What about Marta?' Clive asked his wife, a shade anxiously. 'She may have something planned.'

'Honestly, dear,' Sarina turned on him, 'can't you see Rosanne isn't up to any more travelling today?'

'I just thought—Marta. You know how she'll be just sitting there, waiting.'

'I'll call her, Clive!' Ross McAdam walked up to join them on the verandah. 'She'll be disappointed, but she won't question my decision. How do you feel now, Rosanne?'

'Much better now that my feet are touching the ground.' It was startling to see him with Francine clinging to his arm.

'Well then, that's settled!' Sarina took hold of Rosanne's arm. 'Come along, dear. I expect you'd like to freshen up, and afterwards we'll have lunch.

I confess you're something of a surprise—a little ballerina. What a beautiful colour your hair is. I don't think I've ever seen quite that shade before.'

'You don't know if it's real!' Francine called out teasingly, but Ross answered in his clipped, decisive way.

'I hardly think it's changed since she was a child.'

They went into the house and Rosanne found herself taken over calmly and efficiently as though she was neither physically nor mentally tough enough to look after herself. As she knew from long experience, she was, but she was too sensitive, and too polite to offer any resistance.

By late afternoon she was allowed a short walk around the garden and as the others were still out riding, her hostess immediately offered to keep her company.

'You look much better now you're rested,' Sarina assured her with a genuine concern. 'I really am most dreadfully sorry for you. It must all have been terrible.'

'It was a nightmare,' Rosanne said quietly.

'Such a waste! Robin had potential and he was so very attractive. Can you bear me to talk about him?'

'I'll have to get used to it.' Rosanne stared fixedly at a beautiful parrot that had landed in a gum tree only a short distance away. 'I'm so very frightened Mrs McAdam will hate me for being the one who's alive.'

'My dear child!' Sarina stopped aghast, 'Marta has never hated anyone in her whole life. She's temperamentally incapable of it. I'm appalled you should be worrying this way. Marta is a lovely person, gentle and kind. She'll receive you to her heart.'

'Oh ...' Rosanne tried to smile, 'I should have thought her heart was broken.' She did have an enemy, a *real* enemy who was temperamentally capable of anything.

'Torn to bits at the beginning,' Sarina told her soberly, 'But Ross is a tower of strength. In fact he's her shield against the rest of the world.'

'Her *stepson*?' Rosanne hid her surprise.

'Marta worships the ground Ross treads upon,' Sarina informed her in a definite tone. 'Surely Robin told you?'

'He didn't speak a great deal about his family.'

'I can't believe it!' Sarina's blue eyes flashed. 'A McAdam and he didn't talk about his family and heritage? Of course he was completely uninterested in the land, but still——!'

'Please would *you* tell me,' Rosanne begged. 'You see, I didn't know Robin all that long and I'm sure he would have told me everything in time....'

'Ah, yes.' Sarina patted her arm without quite understanding. 'So where shall I begin? I've known the McAdams all my life. My own people were on the land—still are. My brothers operate six properties to the north-west carrying about fifteen thousand cattle and twenty thousand sheep. We were one of the early pioneering families, but the McAdams were there before anybody. They worked the biggest runs in the Far North. High Valley was carved out of the wilderness and it would go back to jungle if ever they left. Much has been written about the McAdams. Duke McAdam, Ross's great-grandfather, is ranked as one of the North's great nation-builders. He got his nickname from one of the old bushmen much struck by his style and his manners. It stuck to him all his life, though his name was Lindsay.'

'He came out from England?'

'Scotland. A lot of younger sons found their way out here with a strong desire to found their own dynasty. Duke McAdam was no ordinary man and when you're looking at Ross, you'll see Duke McAdam all over again. As a cattle man and a business man Ross has a reputation second to none.'

'And there were only the two boys?' Rosanne was a little startled at the depth of Sarina's allegiance.

'There were four of them.' Sarina stepped closer to the girl, gazing at her intensely. 'Didn't Robin speak of *anyone*?'

'He told me about ... Ross.' Even then she hesitated over his name. 'And, of course, his mother.'

'And he didn't mention his sisters?'

'I never dreamed....' Rosanne replied uncertainly. Though the breeze was warm and aromatic she shivered slightly. How could Robin have kept so much from her?

Sarina sighed and her voice was surprisingly tender. 'Don't upset yourself, dear. I expect you knew Robin had a few problems. No one ever knew when and how it happened. Marta was absolutely indulgent to all of her children. Robin had two sisters, but there was Lyall's influence, his father, and of course, Ross, as his older brother. There was six years between them. Six telling years, I suppose, but Ross really cared about his stepbrother and tried to teach him everything. Unfortunately Robin wasn't a natural, and I fear, at times, he became deeply resentful. Perhaps he spoke to you of it?'

'I thought, or I gathered the impression, he was greatly overshadowed by his stepbrother.'

Sarina did not speak for several moments, then she said in a voice of some bewilderment. 'But really, dear, who can vie with Ross? Certainly poor Robin couldn't. And he could never have taken over from their father, not that there was any question of it at all. Ross's mother brought a fortune to High Valley at a time when its very size was making it unprofitable. Ross was always the heir and with him High Valley has always come first. But Robin never suffered—at least, not from the money angle.'

'Would you tell me about Ross's mother?' All at once Rosanne was filled with a searing inadequacy. She was going to High Valley knowing as little about Robin's family as a complete stranger.

'She died,' Sarina said quietly. 'No life at all, and she was so young and beautiful. I was her best friend and I've never forgotten her; few people who knew her have. She was everything to all of us and so vital, but the gods frowned.'

'What happened?' Rosanne's small face was absorbed and saddened.

'She was drowned in a flash flood, she and the Aboriginal child she was trying to save. Lyall nearly went demented and Jennifer's father had a stroke. She was so precious to all of us and she left her little son. That held Lyall together more than anything else—their son. Marta was Ross's governess until he was sent away to boarding school. She was the only one who could get to him, and it was vital somebody could. She was so quiet and gentle and hardly more than a child herself. Afterwards Lyall didn't bother looking anywhere else. He was done with the frenzy of love and Marta was warm and tender, and of course, she loved him. In time Robin came along, then Julie and Sharyn.'

'And they're still at High Valley?' How awful to have to ask things that she should have been told.

'Julie's married, but Sharyn's still at home and I should warn you, a bit of a handful. Marta ought to have been a great deal firmer with her, but firmness isn't in her at all.'

'And how did Mr McAdam die? Please forgive

me for asking all these questions.'

'But don't you *have* to!' Sarina laid her hand quietly on Rosanne's shoulder. 'Lyall died violently, easy enough on a cattle station. He was handling one of the Brahmans and it went wild. Ross brought it down, but it was too late. You ought to be told Robin was there at the time, but apparently he was paralysed by fear. In times of great danger this can happen to us all.'

'Not Ross.' Rosanne's voice had dropped to a whisper. She felt quite sick.

'I told you, dear, he's no ordinary man. You'll come to see that for yourself.'

By the time they got back to the house, the sunset had turned the sky to a fiery gold and Rosanne hesitated on the verandah looking out at it.

'Stay there, dear, and enjoy it!' Sarina's hand alighted on her shoulder. 'In a few more moments you'll see hundreds of birds flying over.'

'What about you?' Rosanne turned to smile at her.

'I have dinner to think of. Nothing short of the best for Ross and, of course, our little guest.'

Left alone, Rossane looked up at the clarion call of a bird. Just as Sarina had told her, she saw birds flying in a mass, hundreds of them, the fading light throwing back flashes of vivid colour. Where did they settle? It was a wide land, a boundless and, and she was nearing the end of a troubling day.

Why had Robin kept so much from her? She couldn't comprehend it. People in love should share everything and he had told her many times he loved her. Sarina had spoken of his 'problems', and now it was borne home to her mercilessly that Robin had had them. He told her it was impossible to talk confidentially with either his mother or his half brother and for Rosanne, who had longed right throughout her childhood for brothers and sisters, the fact that he had failed to tell her of the existence of either of his sisters was like denying a great gift. Six months she had known him, yet he had told her nothing at all.

With the sun gone, the air was turned to mauve. Such wide open spaces had a wonderful attraction— more, a healing power as one got the importance of one's life into perspective. Rosanne had thought because she was young and still shocked, Robin's tragic death hadn't yet the power to crush her, now she realised her feeling for Robin hadn't gone beyond attraction and an acute desire to be wanted. As a person. There had been little enough love in her life, and love was so important. Poor Robin! He had been so determined she wouldn't meet his treacherous brother. His whole personality had undergone a change on the few occasions he had spoken of his brother. Always brother, never stepbrother. Strange.

Away in the distance she saw the outline of riders approaching the boundary fence, and she found herself standing there until they reached the perimeter of the homestead's grounds and gardens, then she turned away. Presumably Francine was hoping to marry the most eligible man in the North. She looked handsome and confident on horseback, and the vision of Ross McAdam sitting tall and easy in the saddle stayed with her right up until the time she was ready to join the others for dinner. Why wouldn't he be a superb horseman? It would be ridiculous for a man in his position to be anything else.

While she was lingering a little uncertainly, someone knocked on her door, then as she called: 'Come in!' Francine opened the door and stood framed against the light.

'I say, you look different!'

'Do I?' Rosanne lifted a hand to her coiled hair.

'I expect it's because I've used a little make-up.'

'You should do it all the time.' Francine moved across the room, subjecting the younger girl to a raking appraisal. She remembered the big eyes, but with a touch of mascara and eyeshadow they leapt out of a delicately tinted small face, crystal clear and as green as glass. Even the mouth looked different, not childish at all, but damned seductive! Francine had already heard the girl's story from Ross and she had felt sorry for her. But now! Some might even find her enchanting and Francine who usually judged accurately from the start was surprised at her vaguely unpleasant reaction. 'I like your dress, it suits you,' she added a little shortly. And so it did. Cheap, of course, but the green matched the big eyes and added some dangerous subtlety to a too-slender dancer's body.

Used to the sometimes virulent jealousies within a ballet company, Rosanne instantly recognised Francine's expression. Francine had suddenly seen her in terms of female desirability and without a doubt as a possible rival.

'*You* look wonderful!' Rosanne sought to reassure her. After a long afternoon in the sun Francine's fine skin was a deep even gold and she was beautifully dressed in a casual, understated way that spelt money.

'We always dress for dinner,' Francine turned her glossy head to look into the mirror. 'Just how long do you intend to stay with Marta?'

'Just a little while,' Rosanne countered, not knowing whether it was true or even possible. Ross McAdam was dictating the terms.

'I expect as a dancer you can't afford to take much time off?'

'No, it's practice every day. It must be.' Francine was still eyeing her in that disconcerting fashion, so

Rosanne too turned to look in the mirror. This was her Ondine dress, or so Robin had called it; the tiny bodice clinging, the skirt floating. She had always felt good in it, but then she had very few clothes.

'I suppose Robin first saw you at some theatre?'

Did she mean to sound insulting? 'Yes.' Rosanne answered evenly. 'I was dancing in *Coppelia*.'

'Are you any good?' Francine sank on to the canopied bed. Her manner had undergone a change and now she sounded almost aggressively challenging.

'It's been my whole life up to date.'

'I thought good dancers never married or only married people from their own world? Robin must have meant you to give it up?'

'We never got around to discussing it.'

'No?' Francine's hazel eyes were searching. 'Just how long were you engaged anyway? We seem to know so little about you.'

'I couldn't help that.' There was no hint of resentment in Rosanne's voice or manner, but still she disliked the interrogation. 'Robin wanted things that way for a while. He was really a very private person.'

'You mean he had some pretty strange hang-ups.' Francine gave a knowing little laugh. 'He was as jealous as hell of Ross.'

'That's not too surprising, is it?' Rosanne found herself saying. 'I could only guess at Robin's feeling of dispossession, but I know he had one.'

'That's funny! His mother begged him to stay. Marta is a nice person but ineffectual. Not the sort of person one would expect to find as the mistress of High Valley.'

'But she *is*,' Rosanne pointed out quietly.

'At least for a little while longer.' Francine sat up, surprised. 'Ross has enough to worry him without settling all the domestic arrangements.'

'Why doesn't he marry?' Rosanne asked in a tone of indifference.

'He *will*.' Francine smiled a little and put up her hand to stroke her springy curls. 'I've known Ross all my life. My mother was his mother's best friend.'

'Yes, she told me.'

'Then you'll know how very close we are.' Francine got up and smoothed the luminous yellow silk over her trim hips. 'If you're ready we'll go out. Father was mixing us a pre-dinner drink.'

The others were assembled in the lovely old drawing room and Ross McAdam acknowledged Rosanne's appearance with a mocking look. 'Come in, little one, we're waiting for you.'

'What would you like to drink?' Clive Grant-Taylor smiled at her.

'I very seldom do.'

'One won't hurt you,' Francine looked at her curiously, 'or are you thinking of your figure?'

'*Figure?*' her father's eyes began to twinkle. 'Why, a puff of wind would blow her away. She even walks as though she's floating.'

'What about a sherry?' Ross intercepted neatly, his silver eyes shimmering.

'Fine.' Their eyes met and though unnerved by the experience, Rosanne walked towards the cabinet to join him. 'Did you get on to High Valley?' she asked.

'I did.' He passed her the drink. 'Marta is waiting for you with open arms.'

They were momentarily alone as Clive went to attend to his wife and daughter and Rosanne flushed a little angrily. 'I'm glad to hear somebody wants me.'

'Don't underestimate yourself, little one, you're highly desirable.'

'I meant....' she began.

'I know.' His shapely mouth curved sardonically.

'How did the ride go?' Sarina was asking conversationally.

'Splendid!' Francine answered with her eyes on Ross's dark face. He was wearing a stylish shirt and cream linen slacks, and now that Rosanne had to face up to it his sexual attraction was powerful.

Sarina must have been watching her, for there was an odd expression in her eyes. 'I'm so glad you decided to stay overnight, Rosanne. You look so much better.'

'I feel it.' She tried to keep her momentary breathlessness out of her voice. 'I'm only sorry I can't see so much more.'

'Of course you will!' Clive Grant-Taylor eased down on to the sofa beside his wife. 'Ross will bring you back, perhaps for a few days.'

'That would be lovely,' Francine forced a smile, 'but Rosanne has only just been telling me the sooner she gets back to work the better.'

'But surely....' Regret sounded in her father's voice.

'We understand, dear.' Sarina cut her husband off. 'It must be a hard life, being a dancer—the endless practice, the total dedication.'

'Are you, Rosanne?' Ross McAdam asked her, his eyes on her exquisite body, 'totally dedicated to the dance?'

His insolence had her quivering, but she smiled over her flickering temper. Hers was the quiet way and she wasn't going to show herself so easily his victim. 'Sometimes I think the only thing in life is to dance perfectly.'

'And when you're forty and can't move so effortlessly?'

'I hope then that I can teach.'

'How thrilling!' Francine gave a little trill of

laughter that hid her disquiet at the cool intensity of this exchange. 'I took ballet lessons at school, didn't I, Mother?'

'That was just for your deportment,' Sarina smiled fondly. 'There was no question of your considering a career.'

In any case she would have been too tall, Rosanne thought, but didn't say. The conversation became more general, then in a few minutes they went in to dinner.

All through the beautifully prepared and presented meal, Rosanne was made aware of the unspoken understanding between mother and daughter. Something about her appearance had made them review the whole situation. Though it was evident that they both doted on Ross McAdam, it was equally certain they weren't one hundred per cent sure of him. Rosanne understood their feelings, but she could have laughed aloud—the first real laugh in a very long time. Ross McAdam neither liked nor trusted her, and to think of anything else between them sent a shock wave right through her. The only one who really felt kindly disposed towards her was Clive, and his gentle, easy manner released her tongue and kept her nerves from tightening. Though her world was ballet, she read widely for relaxation, so she was able not only to keep up her end of the conversation but contribute something as well.

Afterwards they had coffee on the cool of the verandah and because it was obvious Francine wanted Ross entirely to herself she took a turn around the garden with Mr Grant-Taylor, then excused herself pleasantly. After all, she was only out of hospital and when Francine smiled back at her, she felt she was doing the right thing.

Hours later, because she had slept so deeply that

afternoon, she found herself lying wide awake. The house was very quiet and the lights had gone off long ago. What was she doing here? It was better not to think about it or she would go quietly mad. But there in the velvety, scented dark so many thoughts and images crept in.

He had taken **her** emerald. It made her feel so cheap. The tragedy of Robin was too new to her to allow any analysis of his strange behaviour. Her head told her what she had since heard of him might be true, but her heart refused disloyalties. Poor Robin! He had told her of the intense loneliness of his childhood and that had made a bond between them, but now she had to accept he had the companionship of two sisters younger than himself. Robin. She couldn't begin to understand about him yet.

Moonlight fell across the room, a silver brilliance, and she got up and pulled a matching robe over her thin nightgown. Moonlight had always fascinated her and she was doubly intoxicated by the glorious scents of the bush.

All the main rooms of the house opened on to wide verandahs and her bedroom in the east wing faced a white-latticed garden retreat overhung with a yellow-flowering vine. There were flowering shrubs everywhere, right through the colour range, but at night the beautiful, drowsy grounds were a study in black and silver. It reminded her of a set: Forest at Night.

She was filled with a sudden urge to dance. Could she? Doctor Haarman had told her to be patient, but what did doctors really know about dancers? *Will* made them masters of their bodies. Will and hard work. She had to trust her own instincts, heal herself. Her instinct told her to try something now. If she didn't start moving, it would take an eternity to get back into peak physical condition.

She reached out and held on to the white cast iron lace balustrade. It was too low, of course, for a barre, but she tightened her grip. She had spent weeks in hospital with internal injuries, but miraculously none of her bones had been broken. The thought brought back memories and filled her heart with sorrow, a sorrow that threatened to turn her into a statue. Robin had left her, even in her dreams.

Not far away in a tulip tree, a night bird sang to the moon. It was beautiful, a beautiful song as old as time and it made something flower in her heart. She was alive. She had a future as a dancer. It was the only thing she knew.

One arm came up in a graceful arc as she tilted her body forward and fully extended her right leg back and upwards, upwards, in a classic pose of a ballerina. No pain. She lifted both her arms and executed a few demi-pliés. Not so effortless; no matter. Her anxieties sat more lightly on her than before. Work had always dispelled her worries.

Her long hair, braided for the night, fell loose and the moonlight turned her filmy garments to gossamer shadowing a slight, girl's body. Her lover had left her and she was alone. . . .

Dancers were actors. It was all part of the make-believe. There was a kind of buzzing in her head; the pre-performance hum of a crowded audience; the sounds of an orchestra tuning up. Magic!

She had only been a soloist for a year—one reason why Danielle hated her and had sought to do her harm. Danielle was much prettier, with more flesh on her bones, but still the Director had chosen Rosanne. She couldn't say why, but then she had never seen herself dance.

Oblivious to her surroundings now, made tranquil by the moon, she continued to extend her left leg, then the right. Her audience was invisible, but she knew they were there, would always be there for dancers hundreds of years after she was dead.

The wind blowing through the white jasmine made a sweet, singing sound and she had to tell of her longing. For what? For a lover who held out his arms to her. Not Robin. Being with Robin had been sweet, but there was too much in her, too much unrealised passion, that up until now only dancing had unlocked. Her body really betrayed her, as did her eyes and her mouth. Cool lakes were often deep with turbulent currents beneath the surface.

The end of the verandah was completely shadowed by a climbing rose, the wings of her theatre, and she stood still for a moment just stretching out her hands to the radiance of the moon. Music was inside her, all around. She didn't need the glitter and splendour of a first night; she was just a nymph in the moonlight, not maimed as had been her first terrible thoughts after the accident but still able to float, to elevate, to transcend like the great ones the limits of gravity.

The night breeze had sprung up, swaying the palms in the garden, and immediately her body began to sway with them; her real self, winged in the dark. She whirled, she swayed, traced beautiful arabesques through the silver, bewitched night. Her dancing was perfect, but her lover hadn't joined her, no matter how pleadingly she stretched out her arms.

Suddenly she felt breathless and a funny little cry whirled up from her throat. She had tried to dance too quickly and as she spun to a halt a man suddenly emerged from the shadows and lifted her bodily into his arms.

She wanted to scream, but she could not, and her heart beat ecstatically with the terrible fright.

'Don't you know anything about caution?' he said

to her, and even in the half light his eyes glowed like crystals.

'Oh, *no*!' In an instant her dream world had been ripped apart and she quivered with wrath and resentment.

'You've only been out of hospital two days,' he pointed out bluntly. 'Overdoing it could be a mistake.'

How she wished he had never come! But she was suddenly exhausted and he looked down at her face, then moved the few feet to her room. 'Can't you speak?'

Wouldn't it cause her more misery, yet she tried. 'Why did you wait so long to stop me?'

'Madness,' he said curtly. 'We were both mad together.'

'Then let me down. I can walk.'

'You're more likely to flake out.' He carried her through the French doors and into the room. 'You let out a little cry. Did you hurt yourself?'

'No.' She was utterly disorientated, her heart knocking against her rib cage so frantically it might have been trying to get out. She was used to the feel of a man's arms, wasn't she? Used to being caught and held, yet now her body was stirring in a way that terrified her.

'Please let me down,' she begged.

'You're trembling,' Ross said. 'What are you frightened of? Yourself?'

Her agitation was genuine and she swung upwards in his arms, bringing her face on a level with his own. Her blood had turned molten, but she had to show him she appreciated the game he was playing. 'What are you trying to do to me?' she asked unsteadily.

'*Here*, little one? It would cause a scandal!' Maddeningly his arms tightened and though one half of her wanted desperately to escape him, the other found it so extraordinarily exciting, her hands came up of their own volition to lock behind his head. She hardly knew why she did it, just as she couldn't explain her sudden craving for some physical intimacy between them.

'You're not too particular, are you?' he said in a hard voice that shocked her.

'Oh, God!' He was barbarous, a barbarian. 'Let me go!'

'Not until I know where we both stand. You're extraordinarily seductive for a little bit of nothing, and right at this minute you're out of control.'

'You shouldn't be here in this room,' she said passionately.

'Why not? Don't little ballerinas sleep around? Content in the pleasures of their beautiful bodies?'

'Not *me*!' she said, struggling, but Ross wouldn't let her go. Some note in his voice, some swift sensuality made her realise suddenly she was almost naked —in *his* eyes as they rested on her half revealed breasts.

Resistance was futile, for he only held her closer until she was still. 'All right, so it suits you to play games with me,' she said wearily.

'I thought you were the expert. You know, amusements to pass the time.'

'Yes, they're delicious!' she said bitterly.

'You little bitch!' He moved at last, flinging her on to the bed.

Her heart turned over with fright, yet she sat up and turned her body gracefully into a shaft of moonlight. '*Who's* losing their control?' she said to him. 'I hardly expected a man like you to want to make love to me.'

'Why in hell not? You've got a lovely shell, after all.'

'I've got a spirit too.' He was walking towards her, a tall outline, and Rosanne felt her whole body give a convulsive shudder. She had been right all along. There was a violence in him, a cruel intent, and she had been crazy to provoke him. '*Please....*' she put out a hand to stop him but dropped it as he sank on to the bed. 'It's you who has everything to lose. What would Francine think?'

'Francine is perfect.' He twisted her into his arms and a mad trembling took hold of her. He was insulting her flagrantly, intent on showing up her weakness, and as it happened, she was. Weak ... *weak* ... dominated by his strength and his will.

'Is this how you used to fascinate Robin?' he asked her, skeining her long hair around his hand. 'Pagan supplications before the moon? A little dancing girl at his feet?'

'Robin was never my lover,' she said sombrely. 'You can't understand that, can you?'

'No.' Still he didn't touch her. 'It pleases you to act the little innocent with your big green eyes, but I've seen the truth of you.'

'No, *never*!' She jerked her head and it pulled her hair painfully. 'I never knew you were watching me tonight.'

'But you were pleading for a man?'

'My thoughts were on the dance.' She was shocked at his perception and her breasts brushed his hard chest.

'I know.' He laughed briefly. 'Pretty strong magic, and afterwards...?'

'I told you, I didn't know you were there!' Her slightest movement brought her into closer contact with his hard muscled body.

'Then the moon blinded you.' He lifted his hand and moved it lightly across her breast.

'*Don't!*' It shocked her to the depths of her being.

'You have a very fair skin, haven't you?' he said conversationally, 'almost the colour of a pearl.' With his other hand he stripped off her robe.

'If you don't let me go, I shall scream!'

'You wouldn't dare.' Her flesh was burning where he touched her. 'No matter what you're saying, Rosanne, you'd let me take you.'

'No, not like this.' Her head had fallen back over his arm and she had a feeling of not belonging to herself at all, but to him.

'But dancers are always in danger, aren't they? They tell me it's a very precarious profession.'

His fingers were tracing the fine bones of her shoulder and she wanted to cry out, certain in the knowledge that he was tormenting her deliberately. In reality he hated her though he had begun to see her as a woman.

'You want to punish me, don't you?'

'As a matter of fact, I do!' His silver eyes returned to her face. 'What a pity Danielle isn't here, so you could talk about it in the morning.'

'You don't know Danielle,' she defended herself swiftly, 'the lies she tells.'

'Are they lies?' his low murmur held a supercharged tension. 'I could make you come to me very easily.'

'You couldn't be so cruel. Please, Ross,' she said his name in a wild rush of familiarity, 'this is insane!'

'Don't I know it!' He flung her backwards and her head landed softly in the nest of pillows. 'That was a priceless invitation, but I'm not unscrupulous enough to take it.'

After he had gone, Rosanne turned her face into

the pillows and moaned. She was quivering all over with unreleased emotions and her breasts were aching where his hands had lightly brushed her. What was happening? It was like a dream, and just like a dream she was helpless to handle the situation. Whatever their conflicts, and there were certain to be them, a primitive chemistry worked just beneath the surface.

CHAPTER THREE

NEXT morning they breakfasted early and when Ross's eyes fell on her, Rosanne flinched as if he had struck her. Unwise, because Francine was staring at her.

'Did you sleep well?' she asked.

'Yes, thank you,' Rosanne replied in a faintly stifled voice. In a second of terrible self-revelation she admitted she had lain awake most of the night thinking about Ross McAdam.

'You certainly don't look like it.' Francine poured herself a glass of grapefruit juice and glanced sidelong at Ross. 'I do wish you were taking me back with you. I love High Valley.'

'You're welcome at any time.' He lifted a hand to accept the plate of steak and eggs Sarina had prepared for him. 'Terrific, thank you.' He smiled at her.

'Say when?' Francine swiftly followed up his invitation.

'Could I have another cup of tea?' Clive glanced

down the table at his daughter. 'Let it wait a while, darling. Marta will want Rosanne to herself for a while.'

'I'm so touched she would want me at all.' Rosanne looked up from her plate to give him a strained smile.

Unsmilingly Sarina passed her husband his tea. 'I'm sure Marta has no intention of monopolising you, dear. She's very fond of Francine and if I may say so, having Francine's company will add to the enjoyment of your visit.'

'Give it a week,' Ross suggested, and Francine slanted Rosanne an oblique look of triumph. 'I don't suppose you ride, Rosanne?'

'No.' Rosanne put her knife and fork down. She never had more than juice, cereal and coffee for breakfast and the cooked meal was defeating her. 'I've never had the opportunity, but I love horses. '

'Too much for you, dear?' Clive looked from her plate to her small troubled face.

'I'm sorry. It's delicious, but I can't manage a great deal in the morning.'

'Then leave it. What can I get you?' Sarina stood up quickly and removed the plate.

'Coffee would be lovely.' Behind Sarina's smile Rosanne could sense a coolness and it was making her feel wretched.

The men began to talk about matters affecting graziers and half an hour later, after saying goodbye to Sarina at the homestead, Clive and his daughter took them down to the airstrip in the open jeep. The two girls were sitting in the back and Francine smiled at Rosanne with her lips only.

'Let's hope you don't faint again.'

'I feel very much better.' The wind was whipping at Rosanne's hair and two of the pins that held the loose coil landed in her lap. 'Damn!'

'Why don't you cut it?' Francine was looking at her as if she found so much hair distasteful.

'I'm a dancer, remember.' Loose now, she had to hold the silky ash-blonde fall with her two hands.

'I don't think I could stand all that much hair myself.' Francine continued to stare at her disapprovingly until they arrived at the strip.

Clive helped her out of the jeep and she held on to his warm, kindly hand. He was such a nice man and he seemed to guess at her feelings of oppression. Apparently Ross had made his pre-flight check at dawn, so they were ready to go. The two men shook hands with an obvious wholeheartedness, but Francine seemed intent on making Rosanne feel uncomfortable, though she smiled continually.

'You look nervous,' she commented.

Rosanne had thrown a slightly apprehensive glance towards the plane and she was angry with herself now for doing it. 'I'm not used to light aircraft.'

'You're looking at more than a quarter of a million dollars.'

'Good grief!' Rosanne turned to take another long look at the plane. 'It does look impressive, but so much money?'

'I agree, but Ross isn't going short. In any case, a private aircraft isn't considered a luxury in the Outback. It's a working tool and a way of life. We have a Cessna too, a four-seater. It's locked up in the hangar, but Ross always goes for the top of the range. That's the Golden Eagle. You can't do any better than that, and he brought a party of cattle men with him on the trip down. He's the head of a pretty powerful lobby, the Cattlemen's Union, so it's obvious why he needs executive transport.'

Having all that money to spend still had Rosanne somewhat bemused. 'Do you fly yourself?' She looked up into Francine's golden-skinned face.

'Of course.' Francine half turned away as the men came towards them. 'It seems like you've got a nervous passenger!'

'Come, come, that's not good psychology!' said Clive, looking straight at his daughter. 'Ross is as cool and competent a pilot as Rosanne could ever wish to fly with.'

'Thanks.' Ross glanced sideways at the older man, then clamped a hand on his shoulder. 'I'll be in touch.'

'Good man!'

Rosanne put out her hand, then, liking Francine's father so much, she moved towards him spontaneously, and he leant down and kissed her cheek. 'Lovely to meet you, dear, and we're not going to say goodbye.'

'You're being so kind to me,' she smiled.

'Why ever not?' Clive was clearly enchanted by her youth and her gentle reserve. 'Mustn't hold you up, now. Ross wants to be away.'

The very thought of being alone with him again filled Rosanne with trepidation, but there was nothing else for it but to walk to the plane. Perhaps she should sit in one of the deep comfortable chairs in the cabin and not in the co-pilots's seat. The plane was fitted out with all sorts of options including a stereo eight-track tape player with a headset if she wanted it, and all-round visibility was a joy. Even while she lingered, considering what seat she should sit in, he told her in no uncertain terms 'get up the front!'

The control panel still looked as complicated as ever and she briefly wondered how anyone ever got to flying a jumbo jet. There were gauges everywhere, indicators, alitimeter, magnetic compass, flight instruments, engine instruments, rudder pedals on the floor,

and her eyes flicked over them as the twin turbo-
charged engines sprang into life.

Instinctively she glanced down at Ross's hands on
the control wheel. They were very brown, long-
fingered, and without a doubt, capable. It was a
miracle she had emerged unscathed last night. Had
it really happened? Down on the ground, Clive and
Francine were waving, so Rosanne too lifted her
hand in salute. Her brief stop-over on Malawarra
hadn't been exactly a great success. Ross McAdam,
in at least two people's eyes, was meant for Francine
and woe betide any little opportunist who tried to en-
trap him!

They were moving down the runway now and under full power, the nose lifted off, climbing away
steeply under the effect of a strong headwind.

'Re-lax!' ordered Ross.

'I haven't got much choice.'

'Look down at the view.'

'I don't think Francine likes me,' she said inconse-
quently.

'Do you blame her?'

'I've done nothing!' She looked at him indignantly.

'But spin a web.' His silver glance was challenging,
warning her against provoking another interlude between them.

She stiffened at his implication, wondering what
line of conversation she could get on to that wouldn't
be treacherous. 'I wasn't aware how much money a
plane like this cost.'

'D'you mean you haven't heard I'm a millionaire?'

'Believe me, I don't care about that.' God! she
thought, can I say anything?

'But you thought it over with Robin.'

'Aren't I entitled to a fair trial?' she asked eventually. 'You've condemned me already.'

'On a lot of evidence.'

'You were too willing to believe.' Rosanne drew a deep, uneven breath. 'If you don't need me, I'll go back to the cabin.'

'You *won't*!' Ross caught her wrist. They were cruising now and the noise level was low as befitting such a sophisticated beast. 'Stay and tell me about your life. Start from when you were a little girl.'

'No.'

'*Please*, Rosanne.' He turned to glance at her, and his eyes were so sparkling she gave a sort of groan.

'You're not really interested in hearing my side of anything.'

'But I am. God knows you take some following.'

'There you go again!' she said angrily.

'All right, I'll be quiet.'

'I still remember my parents....' she half shut her eyes.

'How old were you, seven?'

She nodded, not surprised that he knew so much.

'Go on.'

'My aunt didn't want me and she made it obvious right from the beginning. She was much older than my father, her brother, and she didn't really like or understand children.'

'Yet she took you.'

'I didn't say she wasn't a good woman, in her way. She always spoke about her duty and obviously she took it very seriously, but she had no natural—sweetness. It's the only word I can think of. Even when she was trying to be kind she was stern.'

'And it was all so much easier when you started your dancing?'

'Oh yes!' Rosanne cried out in remembrance. 'Right from the very first day I loved it!'

He looked at her and saw the remembered rapture

in her green eyes. 'And of course you were very good?'

'A natural, so my teacher said. She's a wonderful woman. I love her.'

'She's still alive?'

'Oh yes. She runs a big ballet school.'

'Like you intend to?' said Ross with a wry, mocking smile.

She had to ignore him if she was going to continue and after a while she lost herself in telling her own story. How she suddenly awakened to a new life. Always sensitive and imaginative, ballet had brought beauty and magic into her starved little soul. Afterwards, it had brought her a goal, a reason for being: to dance and give pleasure.

She spoke of classes and rehearsals and the iron discipline of the Director. The friendships and jealousies; the fear of chilled muscles and falling. Dancing was dangerous and strenuous, very strenuous, but she loved it, always working to improve.

'And then you met Robin?' he interrupted her.

'He came backstage.' The memory came back vividly. Robin with his fair head and his dark eyes. She had been so sure of his love, yet what Ross McAdam had told her had chilled her. She would never be able to fathom why Robin had betrayed her to his own brother. 'I don't think I'll ever forget!' she said in a soft little voice.

'And in meeting you ruined his whole life,' Ross continued as if he hadn't heard her, and his whole face had darkened.

'God, what a fool I am!' She undid her harness and went to stand up. 'It's no use, is it? You're not going to listen to me, whatever I say.'

He let her go and she moved back into the cabin, taking a seat at the rear. When his mood changed, he was different, dangerous and taut. Rosanne strapped herself in and tried to make herself comfortable. It was going to be a long flight.

Two hours later they touched down at High Valley and Rosanne found herself swallowing convulsively. Malawarra had been pretty impressive from the air, but this place was awesome. It was the tropics, for one thing, and she could see jungle and the jagged purple line of the ranges. The homestead, too, was built at the foot of a jungle-clad mountain and there were so many satellite buildings in a sharp, blinding white that it looked like a frontier town.

Ross hadn't spoken to her except to tell her to adjust her seat and tighten her harness, and she had to force herself to look at him when he came down to her after they had landed. There were people out there to meet them, a lot of them. She had seen that, even from the air, and now he held up her face to him and deliberately looked her over.

'I want you to remember you loved Robin. You fell in love with him and you were going to get married.'

'We were.' It was difficult to answer with his hard hand at her jaw.

'Forget what he wrote,' he said in a sudden anger. 'If you can't ease Marta's suffering, there's one thing you can depend on. I'll get you!'

'You're hurting me.' He was so tall she barely came to his shoulder.

'I will—stake your life on it.' He let her go abruptly. 'Whatever questions Marta asks you, answer like a girl who's lost the man she loved.'

'B-but haven't I?' The colour drained from her heart-shaped face.

'Yet you offered yourself to *me*?'

Rage sent her temporarily insane. He was so tough

and so cruel and so arrogant. She lifted her hand to strike his hateful face, but he caught her wrist and jerked her hard against him. 'You were put to the test, little one, and you failed!'

After that, everything passed in a daze. They were all there to meet her—the McAdams; Marta, her elder daughter, Julie and her husband, Jake. Sharyn glowering at her with Robin's dark eyes. Rosanne hardly heard a word of anything that was said to her; just let herself go with the wave. Behind the family were employees; the overseer, the foreman, office staff, and sitting away on the white timber fence the local men who made up a good part of the mustering teams.

Robin's mother, dressed in a silk shirt and a linen skirt, was a small woman, like herself, and she put her arm around Rosanne's narrow waist and led her away to the car. Both of them had tears in their eyes, though the others had greeted her rather coolly. She was here, like a flying leap into the darkest pit; the dancer's fear of overshooting her little stage and courting disaster.

Behind her she heard Sharyn say in a perfectly audible whisper: 'Hell, she's nothing like we expected.'

They dined that night in the grandest dining room Rosanne had ever been in in her life. A magnificent antique chandelier was somehow dimmed to cast a subtle light and the beautiful paintings and mirrors were complemented by a gold and white wallpaper that accented the richly gilded plaster ceiling. Everything about the house was splendid and there was no way she could ever fit in. It had to be so.

All of them felt burdened by Robin's tragic death, so it wasn't easy to talk naturally. Once again

Rosanne had worn her green dress, because it was the best dress she possessed, and she couldn't help but be conscious of its ordinariness in the muted opulence of this room.

Because it seemed a safe topic, Julie began to ask her about the ballet world. She loved ballet herself and it seemed like she really wanted to hear. Julie was beautiful, a tall, willowy brunette with the McAdam light eyes; the only one to bear a resemblance to her half brother. Sharyn took after her mother, but whereas Marta was of a petite, slender build, Sharyn was very much overweight and compared to her sister, distressingly plain.

One by one they asked questions. All except Ross. He watched her with the narrowed silver gaze she knew now she would have to endure. But her success with Marta was marked. Marta approved of her and though Rosanne was grateful she knew she didn't deserve the warm understanding that shone out of Marta's shy, faun eyes. In a way, she seemed amazingly youthful and so a little unsure of herself, which would explain Ross McAdam's protective attitude towards her.

On the other hand, Julie was slightly impatient with her mother and Sharyn, to Rosanne's way of thinking downright rude. As Francine had warned her, Marta wasn't at all the sort of woman one would expect to find as mistress of a vast estate. She was beautifully groomed and dressed as if she knew she *had* to be, but it was obvious she didn't care for the outward trappings of wealth, neither did she have a masterful personality. The house was run for her by a highly efficient housekeeper Ross had long since recruited and there was no shortage of staff, both for the house and the extensive homestead grounds.

Now a little servant girl, very neat and serious

in a spotless pale yellow uniform, was removing their dinner plates. When she came to Rosanne she glanced sideways and gave a shy smile. Rosanne thought she had never seen such large, glistening black eyes, and the face was exotic; a mixture of races.

'That will do, Nada,' said Julie in a brisk tone. 'Tell Mrs Curtis we'll have coffee in the drawing room.'

'Yes, Miss Julie,' Nada answered in a soft, respectful voice, but when she paused at the sideboard she half turned and gave Rosanne a definite wink. She moved beautifully with great simplicity and grace and Rosanne found herself watching until the girl had left the room.

'What an exotic little creature!' she exclaimed.

'Nada?' Julie looked shocked.

'I suppose she is,' her stepbrother said slowly. 'And she can do a lot better for herself than wait at table, but she's made an unfortunate choice in the man she wants to marry.'

'Why don't you sack him?' Sharyn demanded unexpectedly.

'For one thing he's too good a stockman. For another Nada would follow him wherever he went.'

Rosanne was careful not to look at him. She had always thought Ross McAdam a strikingly handsome man, but here in his own home, master of all he surveyed, she found him too powerful.

As they moved to the drawing room Rosanne paused to look at a cascade of beautiful orchids that had been arranged in a tall Famille Rose porcelain jar, glazed in a design of flowers and figures.

'Like it?' Marta stood beside her, a small, appealing figure.

'It's beautiful. The orchids *and* the vase.'

'I arrange the flowers,' Marta told her a little breathlessly. 'I'd like to show you my bush houses. Of course everything flowers prolifically up here and the orchids grow wild in the rain forests, but I do love growing things in pots and hanging baskets, and so many of them can be brought up to the house.'

'Exquisite!' Rosanne lightly touched the unusual, rose-pink orchid. 'You must be very clever.'

'No, dear, not me.'

'Come on, Mother!' Sharyn turned back to them in irritation. 'Rosanne can see all your orchids tomorrow.'

'I'm looking forward to it,' Rosanne smiled at the older woman, angry with Sharyn for being so short with her mother.

Somehow the evening passed, and Rosanne was glad Julie and her husband would be returning to their own property in the morning. There was a strange curiosity in their eyes when she glanced up to find their gaze upon her. Obviously she was nothing at all like they had expected, which made her wonder what kind of young women had Robin brought home before.

'If you'd like to change your room, you have only to tell me,' said Marta, when they had walked upstairs.

Rosanne shook her head. 'No, it's perfect.' She began to walk to the French doors that led on to the balcony and Marta came to stand beside her. 'I thought you might like to look up at the mountain. It changes all the time.'

'It's very kind of you, Mrs McAdam, to have me.'

'*Marta*—please. I'm not very good at being Mrs McAdam. Never have been.' Marta turned her face away from the contemplation of the floodlit grounds and stared intently into Rosanne's face. Her velvety brown eyes were bright, but the colour had left her smooth-skinned, small-featured face. 'Robin must have loved you very much.'

'He told me he did,' Rosanne said gently.

'You don't know what I've been through!' Tears filled the brown eyes.

'Yes, I do.'

'I'm sorry.' Marta swallowed like a child. 'Of course you've suffered too. We both have. Now that I've met you, know what you look like, I feel easier somehow.'

'I'm glad!' Spontaneously Rosanne kissed the other woman's cheek. There was something pathetic about Marta, something vulnerable and childlike that aroused all her protective instincts. 'Robin spoke to me about you often.' It wasn't true, but she had to say it. 'He loved you dearly.'

'I could always feel it,' Marta said with intensity, 'but Robin never would admit what he really felt. Oh, Robin, Robin, Robin!'

To Rosanne's sorrow she dropped into a chair and burst into heartrending tears.

'Please, Mrs McAdam—Marta.' Rosanne sank to her knees and put her hand on a frail shoulder. 'I'm here to help you. Please let me.'

'Mother, is that you?' Julie's voice sounded in the hallway, then she appeared at the door, looking harassed. 'I've *told* you, Mother, what this would do to you.'

Marta was still crouched over in a desolate fashion and Rosanne found herself patting her very much as she would have done a child. 'Please don't speak to her now.'

Julie's light eyes sparkled and she looked very much like her stepbrother; high-mettled and arrogant. 'I don't like you, Rosanne, telling me when and how I should speak to my mother. She's going to give herself a bad migraine. I know all the signs.'

'I'm sorry,' Rosanne apologised, 'but I just don't think she can help it.'

'*Mother!*' Julie crossed the room and shook her mother's shoulder. 'You'll have to stop this now. You know what the doctor said.'

'Rosanne, are you there?'

'I'm here.' Rosanne answered the mournful voice. 'Can I get you something?'

'You can get Ross,' Julie answered shortly, her fine black brows drawn together, again like her step-brother.

Rosanne sprang to her feet, dismayed by the sobs that were shaking Marta's slight frame. 'Where is he?'

'With Jake in the study.'

At this Marta turned up her head despairingly. 'Please don't go away, Rosanne.'

'She's coming back!' said Julie, her temper rising. 'At the very least, Mother, you should try to pull yourself together, for *our* sakes. You've withdrawn to some place none of us can reach you, and God knows Sharyn needs help.'

Rosanne heard no more. She flew down the stairs on winged feet and when Sharyn saw her, she raised her eyebrows.

'Where's the fire?' she queried.

'Your mother has become distressed,' Rosanne explained.

'Not *again*!' Sharyn put down her glossy magazine. 'You have found yourself mixed up in a pretty situation!'

'Where's Ross?' Rosanne asked with a great effort, appalled by the young girl's apparent callousness.

'I believe he's in the study.' Sharyn picked up her

magazine again. 'I'm certain Mother wasn't calling for me.'

The study door was closed, but Rosanne could hear their voices. She stood very still for a moment, smoothing back her white-gold hair, then she tapped on the panelled door.

'Come in.'

Both men looked surprised to see her, but predictably Ross McAdam spoke first. 'What is it, Rosanne?'

'Your mother—*stepmother*,' she corrected herself in confusion. 'She's upset and Julie wanted me to call you.'

Jake Caldwell was standing and he spread his hands. 'Anything I can do?'

'No.' Ross came around the big carved mahogany desk. 'I expected this to happen.'

Jake saw the distress in Rosanne's eyes and sought to calm her. 'Don't worry, Rosanne. Ross will take care of it. Marta hasn't been at all well and these emotional storms have to be avoided.'

'So why bring me here?' Rosanne directed her question at the big, tough man passing her.

'Why? You don't need an answer to that,' he said curtly. 'Marta loves you already.'

Jake shook his head sadly, looking from his friend's daunting expression to Rosanne's poignant, heart-shaped face. 'It's true. You've given her new life.'

'God!' Ross almost lifted her from the ground. 'Are you coming?'

She wanted to tell him to go to hell like the black devil he was, but she remembered Marta's pleading face.

'You're a savage, do you know that?' She almost shouted at him in her anguish and anger.

'I know, my dear.' He dropped his hard brown hand. 'So come quietly.'

Upstairs in Rosanne's room, Marta was lying stricken on the beautiful bed covering, with Julie standing over her, smoothing the fair hair away from her mother's face.

'*Marta.*' Ross went to her quickly, sank down on the side of the bed and took his stepmother's hand. 'I told you before I brought Rosanne here, you must behave.'

'I know, dear.' Marta sighed and opened her eyes. 'She's lovely, isn't she? In spite of everything Robin picked a girl I can love.'

'Doesn't that ease your heart?'

He was speaking so tenderly, Rosanne couldn't credit it, and the thought came to her that he was a very complex man.

'You're always so good to me, aren't you?' Marta smiled up at him. 'I truly don't want to disappoint you, but I couldn't help it.'

'I know.' He picked up her hand and kissed it. 'But that's enough of making yourself ill. You must live for the rest of us. For a long time.'

'For a *long* time,' Marta repeated. 'You're so compelling, Ross. You were, even as a little boy.'

'So let me take you back to your room.'

'Where's Rosanne?' Marta began to frown.

'Right here.' Rosanne came to stand side by side with the silent Julie.

'Oh, how my poor head aches!' Marta put up a white hand. 'Forgive me, dear, for upsetting you on your first night.'

'Never mind me,' Rosanne smiled at her.

'But I do!' Marta looked back at her intently. 'But for Fate, you would have been a daughter of this house.'

'I think you'd better take Mother to bed,' Julie said in a clipped voice to her stepbrother.

'Come with me. *Both* of you,' Marta said to the girls over Ross's wide shoulder.

Thirty minutes later Marta was settled, but Rosanne's small face was exceptionally white.

'You can do with a brandy!' said Ross when he saw her.

'I'm all right. Is there going to be a storm?' A crack of thunder had already startled her and now she could see lightning illuminating the long windows.

'Don't let it frighten you,' he said.

'How's Mother?' Sharyn ventured into the hallway, a glaze over her dark eyes.

'I think you could have found out for yourself,' said her stepbrother.

'What for?' Sharyn sneered. 'I shouldn't say it in front of our guest, but Mother hasn't let anyone in since Robin died. Only you and now—*her*!'

'Give her time,' Ross replied, almost mildly for such a quick-tempered man.

'I really don't know how much time she wants,' Sharyn said grimly. 'Damn the storm!' She turned and climbed the stairs to her room without saying goodnight.

'I think you'd better have that nightcap now,' said Ross in a crisp voice. 'You look exhausted.'

'I didn't sleep.' It slipped out automatically, though Rosanne would have done anything to withdraw it.

'Oh?' There was a mocking inflection in his sardonic voice. 'Something plaguing you?'

'Don't!'

'All right!' He lifted her pointed chin. 'You're in no danger so long as you act as innocent as you look.'

'That's because I *am*!' She turned her head

slightly, and her loose hair fell over his hand.

'Convince me.'

She coloured violently and pulled away. All the undercurrents were there; the mistrust and hostility, the electrifying attraction. Her own reactions outraged her.

Fortunately Jake came down the stairway and Ross turned his head. 'How about a nightcap?' he asked.

'I think I will!' Jake glanced at both of them, and the chandelier lit up the contours of his lean, good-looking face. 'Julie will be down in a moment. She wanted to have a word with Sharyn—at least if Sharyn will unlock the door.'

'Why is she so unhappy?' Rosanne asked with young solemnity. 'She has so much.'

'The kiss of death to the young,' Ross said cynically. 'I'm afraid Sharyn is much too absorbed in herself.'

CHAPTER FOUR

THE sun woke her.

Rosanne slipped into her robe and walked out on to the balcony. It had stormed during the night, but now the sky was a polished sapphire. There was a mist over the mountain, steam from the warm earth, and she stretched out her slender, bare arms to its jungle-clad splendour. How wonderful it was to have a mountain for a backdrop! The birds were singing a

thousand fanciful songs and their brilliant colours
made splashes of light in the densely green foliage.

So this was High Valley!

The sunlight was dazzling, more intense than anything she was used to, yet it made her feel very happy.
Her skin was very fair, but as a child she had always
tanned to a light gold in summer. Not that the Director would allow it for a minute. A tanned ballerina
would probably be out on her ear.

'How beautiful!' she murmured earnestly.

Below her, rolling away on all sides were lush
green lawns graced with magnificent shade trees and
stands of tall coconut palms. There was a huge
variety of flowering shrubs; oleanders, frangipanni,
golden cassias, hibiscus and bougainvillea, and the
most spectacular flowering vines she had ever seen.
One spilled its brilliant red racemes forty feet from
its support tree down to the ground, and the beautiful
Chilean jasmine, the mandevilla, drenched the whole
balcony in white-flowered sweetness. Even the ram-
pant lantana had been confined to tall banks to bring
in the magnificent tropical butterflies.

It was perfect, she thought, the kind of place
Somerset Maugham should have stumbled upon. He
would have loved the house and its splendidly exotic
setting. Even its owner fitted the picture, a towering
kind of individual at one with his environment.

To her right, beyond one of the great fig trees,
three peacocks came strolling and she blinked her
eyes in astonishment. No one had told her about the
peacocks, and now she looked down unbelievingly at
the glorious, strutting birds. Where had they come
from, and how many of them were there? They were
wandering about now in the morning cool like splendid sultans and one stopped and displayed its gorgeous fan, the brilliant eyes on its tail coverts, before

sedately walking on. How fantastic!

Swiftly Rosanne withdrew from the balcony, holding the silver-gilt hair that had been blowing about her like a cloud. It was only seven o'clock. Plenty of time to explore. Whoever heard of peacocks wandering about the garden, the sunlight glowing on their iridescent feathers. She almost ran into the shower, as though if she delayed too long the birds would disappear.

Afterwards it wasn't difficult to decide on what to wear. She had very few clothes, but the voile sundress in deep green with blue and gold flowers in a wide border around the hem seemed to match the lavish colouring of the birds. It had cost her around twenty dollars, but she had a priceless asset going for her that she too often tended to disregard; a beautiful graceful body that men's eyes tend to follow.

A strange excitement was gathering in her and when finally she looked in the mirror she was startled by the animation in her expression. She hadn't looked like this in a long time. Robin's death had changed her life violently. It had brought her to High Valley, and now she began to study the face that had never interested her a great deal before.

She was plain, wasn't she? Her aunt had insisted she was plain. *Plain little thing, Rosie, not a bit like your father!* She considered her profile this way and that. Her eyes seemed to fill her face and they were green instead of blue. She had always admired blue eyes and her aunt had once told her green eyes were not to be trusted. Reluctantly her mouth twitched. Once could scarcely credit that.

Her cheekbones were wide, too wide perhaps, narrowing down to a pointed chin. At least her skin was good and although her aunt had thought her dark eyebrows and lashes 'theatrical' with her ash-

blonde hair, she couldn't see that this was exactly so.
They gave definition to her face and made her eyes
appear more brilliant. Her head tilted, she ran her
fingers down the clean line of her jaw and throat. She
could almost feel Ross McAdam's hard fingers holding her chin.

What a brute! Here was no liar, no schemer, no
Circe, surely? She was just an ordinary girl with a
gift for the dance. Quickly she turned away from her
own image and stood poised in the centre of the
room. Robin's touch had never troubled her, igniting
a flame of sensuality. Now she could only think back
to the moment when a man's fingers had lightly
touched her breast.

All kinds of sensations stabbed at her and she even
bent over. Robin had been so gentle, considerate,
aware that she was a virgin, not a ravishing bucca-
neer. Yet Robin had betrayed her. It was so very,
very strange.

No one was about when she went downstairs, but
she could hear the muffled sounds of voices and the
clatter of crockery from the vast kitchen that was
separated from the main house by a covered walkway. She had met the housekeeper, Mrs Curtis, very
briefly and found her quite formidable; a dragon of
a woman who dominated the staff, cooked like a
great chef and apparently ran the household like
clockwork. Marta obviously had no talent for such
things and no aspirations either. Indeed it had seemed
to Rosanne that the mistress of High Valley went in
some awe of her own housekeeper.

Out in the garden, the birds were squabbling or
making love in the beautiful native trees and even as
she looked a dozen or so whirled out of the leaves to
flash their painted plumage before diving back into
the nectar-laden flowers. It was all so incredibly

lush, and after she walked a short distance, she turned to look back at the house. Yesterday she had been so nervous, so hideously unsure of herself she hadn't been able to truly appreciate her surroundings; now her eyes lingered on the external façade of the large white house.

It was an excellent example of timber architecture at its best and its superb verandahs were ideal for the tropics. She particularly liked the design on the white cast-iron panels that blended so beautifully with the carved caps and fretwork of the wood. It was a romantic house in an undeniably romantic setting, and her eyes went beyond the house to the mountain that was covered with rain forest.

They called it Eagle Rock and there was an old mine up there hidden by the lawyer vines and the giant tree ferns. It was still the pre-monsoon period, but in the Wet, Julie had told her, the mountain stored up so much moisture that even in the Dry the forest floor was cool and damp. There were orchids up there, too, though no one had gathered them for a long time. Orchids and great fan palms and the golden bower-birds. Rosanne could imagine their brilliant spots of colour in the mysterious green glens.

The peacocks seemed to have disappeared, but there were so many banks of shrubs they could well be resting lazily in the shade. She moved on, attracted by the size of a magnificent poinciana. It was heavily in bloom and as she stood beneath it, looking up, her heart nearly stopped in shock.

'Golly!' the schoolgirl exclamation broke from her, but she was frozen to the spot. A snake was sliding down one of the main branches and as she shuddered in horror it slid out its long, slender, forked tongue.

She had always hated snakes, though she had never

been a yard away from one in her life.

'Help!' she called to anyone, though the garden was empty. The snake was still gliding silently down towards her, while she stood there petrified with fright. Of course Eden was alive with snakes. All sorts of snakes—tree snakes, black snakes, brown snakes, copperheads, death adders, taipans. Australia had some of the world's deadliest snakes. This one had a cream belly.

'Rosanne?'

She heard Ross's voice call her, still she couldn't stir. If she frightened the snake it might drop on her.

'What the devil——' He was beside her, arrested by her stricken pose.

She could speak now, but her voice was full of tremors. 'It's a snake. I hate snakes.'

'Where?' He lifted his arrogant head and frowned.

'Right above your head.'

Instead of registering alarm, he laughed. 'I can see I'll have to spend a little time telling you which snakes you have to watch for.'

'My spine's crawling,' she whispered, 'yet I can't move.'

'Well, I don't really mind carrying you in to breakfast.'

She closed her eyes and when she opened them again they were well clear of the tree and Ross was staring into her face. 'This is going to be sheer hell for you,' he said softly.

'What is?' Did she *have* to fall into his arms?—especially when now she recognised the danger.

He clicked his tongue. 'What indeed!'

'Oh, Ross——'

'*Rosanne*,' he mocked her swiftly. 'It almost sounds as though you were made for me.'

'Let me down!' she begged.

'Oh, I see, the little game's over.'

'You're crazy if you think I'd play games about snakes!'

'It was absolutely harmless,' he returned smartly.

'Of course I knew that all along.' Her green eyes flashed vividly and she put her hands up on to his shoulders and propelled herself quickly and gracefully out of his arms.

'That was clever!' he said admiringly of her jump. 'Tell me, did you sleep well?'

'Thank you, yes.' In her sandals she felt smaller than ever beside this suave, arrogant man. 'I never dreamed anywhere could be so lovely.'

'You're still sticking to your story, then?'

She lifted her head with a start. 'I don't understand?'

'Robin never told you a thing. Not a thing.'

'No,' she said in frustration.

'He was going to marry you, yet he told you nothing.'

'He told me about you!' She stopped abruptly and looked up at him. 'And he didn't tell me a darned thing that wasn't true.'

'Like what?' he mocked, his mouth curling slightly. Today he was wearing a blue denim shirt and narrow jeans, yet he still looked intriguingly elegant.

'You know it won't do any good talking about it.' She looked away from his silver eyes. 'I saw peacocks in the garden, didn't I?'

'Uh-huh, change of subject!' Unexpectedly Ross grinned. 'Yes, little one, you did. They roost along the creek, but they often wander into the garden.'

'They're gorgeous,' she said.

'You mightn't think so when you hear them shriek. But wait until I'm handy, then you can jump into my arms again.'

'For a start, I never have.'

'Dear Jehovah!' he sighed.

Sharyn was waiting on the verandah and when they got closer, Rosanne smiled up at her. 'Good morning.'

'Where have you been?' Sharyn fixed her with a stare.

'It was far too beautiful a morning to stay in bed.'

'Oh, I know!' Sharyn looked suggestively from one to the other. 'Ross always gives his guests special treatment.'

'Thanks, Sharyn, you're such a pet.'

Sharyn flushed to the eyebrows and Rosanne was inclined to feel sorry for her. 'As a matter of fact, I wandered off by myself,' she explained, still smiling. It was difficult not to be aware of Sharyn's antagonisms and evidently she was jealous of anyone her half brother took a slight interest in.

'All right, let's go in to breakfast,' said Ross, 'and afterwards I'll have to take myself off. Marta is certain to have made plans for the day.'

'Oh, my God!' Sharyn tripped a little clumsily and Rosanne caught at her arm. She didn't know why Sharyn was making her mother such a target for her irritation, but it wasn't too long before she was to find out.

Julie and her husband left a short time after breakfast, Julie with a slightly troubled face, and Rosanne felt conscious of Marta's clinging to her arm. This morning Marta looked very frail, but there were lamps in her eyes and an evident eagerness to extract from Rosanne's company the healing elixir she needed. It was odd, then again not so very odd that it should be a stranger to whom Marta should turn in her need. Robin had been her only son and Rosanne was the means of bringing him back to her if only in memories. It was touching and it was some-how a burden.

When later Marta suggested a tour of her bush houses, Rosanne was embarrassed and bewildered to find Sharyn had not been included. Left alone with the girl for a few moments she wondered if she dared say what she was feeling. Sharyn had settled into a planter's chair on the verandah, looking straight ahead, but with an odd, half angry expression on her flushed face.

'Please don't resent me, Sharyn,' Rosanne said softly.

'Oh, don't mind me. Why the devil should I resent you?' Sharyn fumbled in her pockets and withdrew a packet of cigarettes. 'It's Mother who doesn't want me to tag along.'

'It's a very difficult time for her.'

'I'm afraid everything is difficult for Mother.' Sharyn lit a cigarette and inhaled deeply. 'She and Robin fought for years. Now he's dead she's acting as if she'd give the world to have him back.'

'I'm sure she would.' Rosanne said quickly. 'Robin was her only son.'

'Then we can all be thankful she didn't have any more.'

'What do you mean?' Rosanne looked down at her startled.

'Oh, let's forget about Robin,' Sharyn shrugged. 'He never interested me very much.'

'I can't believe it.' Rosanne turned to look out over the garden. 'I would have given anything to have had a brother.'

'Not like Robin,' Sharyn said emphatically. 'It might be you didn't know him very well at all.'

'Well, my dear, here I am!' Marta came out on to the verandah smiling, but her look changed when her eyes fell on her daughter. 'Darling, must you persist with that filthy habit?'·

'I must,' Sharyn said doggedly.

'You know I utterly disapprove, and so does Ross.'

'Oh, bosh, Ross likes a cigarette too. Anyway, I've got to do something to lose weight.'

'I'm afraid smoking isn't the answer,' Marta said. 'How you can sit there undermining your health!'

'Perhaps you'd like to join me when I limber up,' Rosanne suggested mildly.

'I don't think so. I hate exercise.' Sharyn returned rather too fast. 'Don't let me keep you on such a splendid day.'

'Oh, Sharyn!' Marta looked at her with soft, reproachful eyes.

'You're not by any chance asking me to come along, are you, Mother?' Sharyn asked challengingly.

'You mustn't mind, dear,' said Marta. 'Just for today I want Rosanne to myself.'

'I hope you can stand it, Rosanne.'

What an extraordinary girl! Rosanne turned away a little shocked and Marta came down the stairs to join her. 'Sharyn needs an interest,' she said confidingly. 'Everyone needs an interest in life.'

'Really? It seems such a wonderful life here at High Valley.'

'It's the only thing that has ever interested the McAdams, but I'm not really a McAdam and neither are my children, except Julie. She's a McAdam— strong, clever, confident people.'

'But you're happy here, aren't you?' Rosanne looked into Marta's thin, fair face.

'I—I don't know. I don't know anything any more.'

She looked so momentarily unhappy Rosanne began to dread what might happen. 'Life will come right again, Mrs McAdam. You must believe it.'

'*Marta*, dear.' The soft voice was rough with emotion. 'All my life on High Valley I've never really thought of myself as Mrs McAdam. There was only one Mrs McAdam—Ross's mother. Really, I mean it. I know I can tell you just what comes into my head. I was so young, inexperienced. I adored my husband, but I was never in any doubt as to why he married me. Who could look at me after Jennifer? I used to so hate the way people compared us. They didn't think I knew what they were saying, but I did.'

'I'm sure you're too sensitive,' said Rosanne.

'Lyall often used to go off alone and stay away for days,' Marta went on. 'He was always alone, quite alone, in the wilderness. Later on, of course, he took Ross. He lived for his son.'

'He had two sons,' Rosanne said.

Marta picked a deliciously scented tuberose and held it to her face. 'The trouble was Robin was very nervous of his father—and then he was allergic to horses.'

'*Robin* was?' The surprise showed on Rosanne's face. 'He told me he loved them. How he used to win prizes and so forth.'

'Poor boy!' Marta threw the flower away and picked another. 'Ross learned to ride while he was learning to walk, but Robin developed a most distressing allergy almost from the beginning. The plain truth was he was more frightened of horses than he was of his father. Lyall never did understand, and I'm afraid he let his contempt show.'

'How terrible!' whispered Rosanne.

'No, Lyall wasn't a cruel man. He was simply a MacAdam, and he was shocked at his own son's deficiencies. Ross and Julie just took to everything that was expected of them like ducks to water, but my other two. . . .'

'Couldn't someone have helped Robin? I mean, there are anti-histamines and all sorts of things.'

'It was an emotional allergy, so we were told. He couldn't compete with his stepbrother and he was too frightened to try.'

'And what did Ross do about all this?' Rosanne asked with faint anger.

'He did everything he possibly could to help his brother,' said Marta. 'Don't think Ross didn't try. He was always watching out for his young brother, and Robin idolised him, of course. Idolised him—and I suspect hated him at times. Ross was just too much his superior in everything and human nature being what it is, my poor boy was jealous.'

'You must have had a good many worries,' Rosanne murmured, thinking how it must have been.

'Oh, I did.' Marta's delicate nostrils were pinched and hard. 'I hated Robin being away from us at all. I missed him terribly.'

Yet you didn't get on, according to Sharyn, Rosanne thought, but couldn't say. They were approaching the bush houses and she sought to lighten the conversation. 'I'm really looking forward to seeing your orchids.'

'Oh, I grow other things!' said Marta more happily. 'My one talent, I've a green finger.'

'That *is* a talent,' Rosanne replied sincerely, thinking of her failures with indoor plants. 'I was hoping to see the peacocks again.'

'*Those* creatures!' Marta reacted unexpectedly. 'I hate them, especially when they start screaming. It's like someone being strangled.'

'But they look so magnificent!'

'One chased me once!' Marta was opening the

latticed door of the bush house and Rosanne caught a glimpse of her face. It was white with remembered fright. Marta was a timid woman in many ways and life wasn't easy for timid people.

But inside the bush house it was a fantastic, sheltered world. There were plants everywhere. Tropical orchids and bromeliads; on the ground, on the long benches and hanging from the rafters in a variety of baskets and old fern bark.

'How marvellous!' Rosanne ventured further into the warm, moist shade house. 'I though orchids were difficult to grow.'

'Not here, dear. Orchids are denizens of the jungle, you know. A lot of these have come from Malaysia and they're doing extremely well. You've missed the flowering of the State flower, the dendrobium, the Cooktown orchid. It flowers in the cooler months and it's not really hardy outside the tropics, but there are plenty more.'

'I can see that.' Rosanne's expression was rapt. There were flower spikes everywhere in a wide colour range and Marta, seeing her interest, began to point out the different species, the kind of treatment she gave them, and their country of origin.

For more than an hour she lost herself going from bush house to bush house, showing her wonderful bromeliads and a vast assortment of tropical cacti and succulents. The night-blooming cereus from Mexico had been planted out in the garden where it rambled up a tall tree and Marta told her, 'any moonlit night now, I'm expecting it to bloom.'

She seemed much happier than when they had started out, but just as Rosanne began to relax inevitably the conversation came back to Robin.

'Why didn't you tell me, dear?' Marta said suddenly, a brooding expression in her eyes.

'It was what Robin wanted.'

'But the most natural thing in the world would have been to tell me,' Marta persisted. 'I mean, I'm not a dreadful person. We're so comfortable together.'

'Please believe me, Mrs McAdam—I mean, Marta —I wanted to tell you at once, but Robin had his own reasons for wanting the delay.'

'But *months*?' Marta asked humbly, and shook her head from side to side. 'Robin was so close to me as a child, then these last few years I only seemed to enrage him. Of course you knew he had a temper.'

'He couldn't have been more gentle to me.' Except for that one time after André, and Rosanne had tried to push that to the back of her mind.

'I'm glad.' Marta took her hand. 'You're such a gentle girl yourself. You loved him very much?'

'Yes.' A strange sort of self-loathing was on her. She didn't want to face it, but she had to. She had never loved Robin, not the way she had found she could feel in a minute. Just the brush of another man's fingers had shown her that. It was shocking and so utterly disloyal to Robin's memory that the tears sprang into her eyes.

'There, there!' Marta pressed her hand, unexpectedly the strong one. 'I didn't want to upset you, dear. I just wanted to know.'

'It's all been such a terrible shock.'

'I know.' Marta's face showed her own agony. 'I couldn't bear you not to be cared for—Robin's fiancée, the girl he loved. I believe you have no one?'

'Not for some time now,' said Rosanne in a lowered voice. Wasn't that what had precipitated her involvement with Robin? The fact that she had no one. Even Robin had called her Little Orphan Annie.

'How long can you stay with me?' Marta asked,

and flushed painfully. 'It's such a comfort having you here.'

'Until you're feeling much better,' Rosanne promised.

Marta smiled, and it was a lovely sight. 'I must get Ross to organise something so you can meet people. But for a cruel stroke of fate you would have been my daughter-in-law, and I take some peace out of the fact Robin chose you. It's a tremendous relief to find you such a lovely creature.'

'*Me?*' Rosanne's flawless skin went pink.

'Surely you've been told that, dear, often enough. That cloud of hair and that white skin and your beautiful eyes. Yes, you're beautiful, and Ross has told me very gifted.'

'Which reminds me, for as long as I stay I'll have to keep in practice,' Rosanne managed in some bewilderment. Surely Marta had to be pretending to find her beautiful, yet there was no shadow of pretence in her eyes.

'We'll arrange something.' Marta glanced at Rosanne's very slender figure. 'I don't think Sharyn will join you, but I wish she would. She's putting on much too much weight for her small frame, but I can't seem to discuss anything with her these days. She didn't used to be so rude and ungracious, but she seems to be going through a difficult stage. Julie was always so beautiful, Sharyn tends to think of herself as an ugly duckling. I should know, I was an ugly duckling myself.'

'What nonsense!' Rosanne couldn't help saying it.

'Very different from Jennifer!' Marta gave a bleak little smile. 'There's a portrait of her in the gallery.'

'Not the woman with the dark hair?'

'Yes, indeed,' Marta said dryly. 'Jennifer was extraordinarily beautiful and so vital sometimes I think she's even alive today. There was a time I would have loved to have taken that portrait down. It used to be in the drawing room, but Lyall couldn't bear to hide it altogether. How extraordinary men are! Days before he died he told me he'd seen Jennifer picking flowers at a waterhole.'

'How strange!' Rosanne felt a shiver go up and down her spine.

'He said she smiled at him.'

Rosanne didn't answer, couldn't answer, and after a minute Marta walked on. The warm air blew perfume in their faces, but the enchantment had been brushed with disquiet. There were all sorts of tensions in this tropical paradise and right at that moment Rosanne felt hemmed in by them.

Ross didn't return for lunch, but at mid-afternoon he put in an appearance. Marta, who seemed in indifferent health, was resting quietly in her room for an hour and Rosanne and Sharyn were lounging beside the pool indulging in a very small turn of conversation. Sharyn was prickly and sarcastic and obviously intended to stay that way.

'Well, hello!'

Rosanne hadn't been expecting him and she sat up quickly in the shade of the white-fringed umbrella. Although she had brought a swimsuit she never wore a cap, so her long hair was wet and plastered to her back.

'Where did you spring from?' Sharyn questioned.

'I thought I'd take Rosanne for a turn around. Want to come?'

'It's too hot.' Sharyn gave him a withering look.

'So you get more lethargic every day. But who cares? Brad won't.'

'Would you *mind*!' Sharyn cried. 'I have absolutely no interest in Bradley Parker.'

'Tell him that when he comes back, Sharyn baby,' Ross mocked her. 'You always have tried to hide your head in the sand.'

'So when are you going?' Sharyn asked pointedly.

'What sort of thing would amuse you anyway, Rosanne?' He turned his attention away from his bristling young stepsister.

'I think I'd like to see the horses.'

'Good God!'

'Well, you did ask me.' Already Rosanne was feeling agitated. He was wearing a pearl grey Stetson, a look that was quite new to her, and it made him look quite shockingly devil-may-care and attractive.

'All right, fair enough. How long will it take you to put some clothes on?'

'A minute.' She was vaguely exasperated by the look in his eyes. Sharyn's bikini was a lot briefer than hers was.

'Go to it, then, girl!' he called after her. 'Make it jeans and I'll throw you up on old Lightning's back.'

'You're not telling me she can't ride?' Sharyn enquired with cheerful contempt.

'You never know what you can do until you try.'

In the end, Rosanne didn't have to try very hard, for it seemed she was a natural. Even Ross McAdam had to recognise it, for he lifted her off the mare and rubbed his chin.

'Are you sure you've never been on a horse before?' he asked.

'Actually I've never stood close to one in my life.'

'Then I reckon if we can persuade you to stay a month or two you'll make a very passable rider.'

'It's kind of you to say so.' Under her banter Rosanne was rather thrilled and excited. It wasn't so strange to be up on a horse, in fact she liked it very much. 'I think I could find my way around on this gentle old lady.' Curly, the groom, had passed her a lump of sugar and she offered it to the mare.

'On the subject of finding your own way around, forget it,' Ross answered directly. 'Wherever you go, you'll have to be watched.'

Curly, the Aboriginal groom, laughed heartily and Rosanne found herself saying a little indignantly: 'I've been looking after myself for a long time.'

'Sure!' Curly's boss scoffed at her. 'Only up here, we're going to watch you like a hawk.'

'Yes, miss,' Curly seconded cheerfully. 'Now I could ride around with me eyes shut. We locals are the only ones that know the country, except the boss here. He loves it. Really loves it, like us.'

'Haven't you got something to do?' Ross asked the man dryly.

'Sure, Boss!' Curly walked to the mare's head. 'I don't want to work for no one else but you.'

'And not too much of that either!'

They watched the man swing up into the saddle, still smiling broadly, then dropping a hand on her shoulder, Ross turned her away. 'Well, you've made a start. All you need now is to do some riding each day.'

'Oh, look,' she breathed. 'There are the peacocks again!'

'Nothing to worry about.' He looked at her.

'Who's worried?' She threw him a brilliant green glance. 'They're beautiful!'

'I'm glad you think so. They've frightened the hell out of some of our guests.'

'However could they do that?'

'Oh, sometimes they rush a likely-looking victim or they let out a bloodcurdling scream when they're disturbed.'

'Oh,' she laughed, and swept back her drying pigtail. 'If they make a rush at me I'll just wave my hands.'

'You're unexpected, aren't you?' he commented suddenly.

She looked up at him to find his dark face unreadable. 'And you'd rather be able to sum me up all at once?'

'I usually do.'

'That would be the best way, wouldn't it, but you don't know me at all.'

'And I've a deep distrust of green eyes.'

'Don't *say* that!' A shiver of resentment knifed through her.

'Why not?' The glint deepened. 'Green eyes hold secrets. Too many secrets.'

'I don't think I'm old enough for all those secrets,' she said. 'You can't imagine what you're like when you change. You were almost friendly before.'

'I suppose you could say I didn't want to frighten Lady.'

'I thought you said her name was Lightning?'

'My dear girl,' he smiled in his exasperating manner, 'Lightning would keep anyone at bay. He's thrown more people in the last year than any other horse I can remember. You were up on Lady.'

'At least she liked me.'

'Well, you weren't exactly a great weight on her back. Now do you want to see some of the property or don't you?'

'Yes.' She didn't know where it would lead, but she wanted to.

'Then we'll take the jeep. I'd like you to relax because Marta will want to talk to you some more.'

'She's already talked to me,' she said awkwardly.

'Do you think so?' This time Ross turned on her so she had to halt abruptly. 'Believe me, little one, the subject of Robin isn't closed.'

CHAPTER FIVE

A WEEK went by on a sort of a glory wave. Life on a great station was full of excitements and Rosanne, so young and empty of experience beyond the strict world of the ballet, found her new life a wonderful experience.

In the morning she rode, and then again in the afternoon. She was very much improving, but she still couldn't call herself a horsewoman. Sometimes Sharyn rode with her, her moods alternating between a strangely shy friendliness and a prickly aggression, or Curly trailed behind her as her watchdog. There was something very endearing about Curly, and behind the merry grin, a quiet dignity.

High Valley spread away from them in all directions; wide grasslands, wild jungle, tangled lignum clumps, lovely lagoons where they could see their clearcut reflections quivering in the spaces between the floating waterlilies, a thousand places that gave the uninitiated Rosanne infinite pleasure. All about them too lay the old hunting grounds and the sacred ritual areas of Curly's tribe, and as soon as he saw Rosanne was genuinely interested rather shyly he rode alongside her and told her many stories of his ancient race. There were spirits of the bush everywhere and Rosanne too could feel them falling under the powerful influence of the vast untamed land. The Dreamtime legends were countless and often so beautiful and imaginative Rosanne could even see herself dancing the legend of the bird goddess, Brilyah.

Many miles away across that luxuriant, rugged landscape High Valley came down on the Gulf where the mangroves grew in thick forests and the coral reefs were covered in seaweed. Rosanne would have loved to penetrate that far, to see the turquoise blue water, but there was only one person who could take her and that was Ross. She had only been there a week, yet already she knew he worked a long, hard day; up at dawn and home by sundown. There were so many matters claiming his attention, so many other activities associated with being a top cattleman; work seemed to carry on into the night with consultations with his overseer and office staff. The woman who loved him would have to live his life entirely. The thought occurred to Rosanne many times and each time she thought of Francine. Francine was perfect. Hadn't he told her? She could ride and shoot and fly a plane. She understood about the land and Rosanne was certain she wasn't frightened of snakes.

The men seemed to have accepted her. She had smoko twice at the camp sites, suddenly loving billy tea and a freshly baked damper. The camp cook was a Chinese man, and he had somehow produced for her a bone china cup and saucer, though she wouldn't have cared if she too had to drink out of a mug. They all seemed very content and happy, and when it was time to leave, they all doffed their hats to a man.

Rosanne, who had never been allowed a pet since her parents had been taken from her, found the abundance of animal life fascinating. Apart from the endless stream of cattle, hundreds and thousands of them, there were the horses and a brumby herd she and Curly had disturbed one day. The kangaroos were beautiful, staring across at her with their mild large eyes, the emus and the turkeys, the prolific bird life, even the giant lizards with their writhing armoured tails. Anyone foolish enough to disturb a crocodile had to be prepared to pay for it, but Curly always told her which lagoon not to go near. Perhaps she would see one and slink away in fear.

'Crocodile, dangerous, miss,' Curly told her unnecessarily. Months before a stockman had been taken in the Territory and the horror lingered.

Finally one morning, Sharyn's curiosity overcame her and she ventured into the large empty room that had been set aside for Rosanne to practise. To her surprise, Ross had had one of his men rig up an excellent makeshift barre and she was already achieving a good measure of her old control.

Lost in her own efforts, it took a few minutes for her to become aware of Sharyn's presence, then she broke off to give Sharyn a sweet, uncomplicated smile. 'It's not as easy as it used to be!'

'You would have fooled me.' Sharyn sauntered further into the room looking Rosanne critically up and down. 'You're just a wisp of a thing, aren't you?'

'In my leotard,' Rosanne smiled. Her hair was coiled tightly on the top of her head, but some silky streaks clung to her hot cheeks.

'Do you think you could do anything for me?' Sharyn demanded suddenly.

'In what way?' Rosanne reached over and touched the younger girl on the shoulder.

'Oh, you know, get rid of this flab.' Rather defiantly Sharyn turned round and faced the mirror. 'Just look at me, I'm horrible!'

'It wouldn't take long to fine down.' Rosanne took care not to stand beside Sharyn to incite her further.

'What would I have to do?' Sharyn asked.

'Watch your diet. Stick to a series of exercises I'll give you.'

'Will you do them with me?' Sharon frowned at her own reflection, then pulled a face. 'I've got no discipline at all.'

'Well, it's not easy,' Rosanne said soothingly.

'The dear old good fairy gave all the looks to Julie,' Sharyn said. 'She's really beautiful, isn't she?'

'She is.' Rosanne returned to her drill. 'But you have your own image. Petite blondes are always appealing.'

'Like you,' Sharyn echoed moodily. 'The truth is no matter how much I try I'm putting on weight.'

'Ah no,' Rosanne dared to be frank. 'Sugar is the enemy, and you've got a sweet tooth.'

'Would you stop bending there for a minute. No wonder you've got such a tiny waist!'

'Sure.' Rosanne picked up a towel and wiped her face. 'If you want me to help you, I'll be very happy to.'

'Julie's never had to diet in her life,' Sharyn sighed.

'Maybe she runs through life.' The little Rosanne had seen of Julie she was sure she did very little sitting around. 'Do it for Brad.'

Sharyn tensed. 'That jerk!'

'Then you really don't care for him?' Rosanne didn't know anything of this Brad at all except that the very mention of his name made Sharyn fire.

'Yes, I *do*!' Sharyn threw her hands violently above her head. 'And I intend to get him.'

'Atta girl!' Rosanne couldn't help laughing. At any rate she was making progress with Sharyn. 'You're going about that the wrong way,' she pointed out, watching Sharyn's downward swing. 'One can't achieve fitness in one session. Today you can even

bend your knees. And oh, another thing—you'll have
to wear a leotard. I'll lend you one of mine.'

Unexpectedly Sharyn burst out laughing and without her sulky expression she looked a different girl.
'Do you mean to say you think it's possible I might
fit into it?'

'I have a feeling you soon will.'

'Don't hold your breath!' Sharyn replied flip-
pantly, but Rosanne could see the quick pleasure in
her face. It meant Sharyn was going to try.

After that, the limbering up went on every morning, though Rosanne had to recognise that Sharyn
was basically lazy and need a strong incentive to keep
up her efforts. A few days on a diet hadn't improved
her temper, but both Marta and Rosanne were
pleased and relieved to see she kept to it. Marta had
even overcome her reluctance to approach Mrs
Curtis asking for special meals, but that lady, un-
usually bone-thin for a chef, had been almost graci-
ous, insisting: 'You must leave everything to me,
madam.'

Something had to happen to bring the curiously
peaceful interlude to an end, and the following
weekend Francine arrived. Rosanne didn't see her
until late afternoon, having taken the horses some
distance with Curly and Nada, the little housegirl,
who had appeared on the scene just as they were leaving.

It was a beautiful afternoon with phantom riders
and cattle swimming in a sea of mirage and the company of two very gentle brown people who understood their environment in a way few white men ever
could. Both of them rode effortlessly and Rosanne,
happy in their company, didn't notice that they kept
their eyes about them constantly, interpreting every
sign that could mean danger.

'Look, did you ever see anything like that, miss?' Nada pointed a thin brown arm to the sky. 'All those clouds tumblin' colour.'

'It's a message,' Curly looked up at the radiant haloes, 'de' Wet's comin'.'

As they rode back towards the homestead, they saw the Cessna coming in and a short time later it left.

'Miss Francine!' Nada whispered, and her great black eyes looked profoundly disturbed.

'Why, what's the matter?' Rosanne glanced quickly into the exotic little face.

'Nada nearly goes hysterical when Miss Francine arrive,' Curly explained. 'Miss Francine don't bother about the likes of us. Coloured girls are got leprosy.'

'I'm sure she doesn't mean anything,' said Rosanne.

'I'm bloody sure she does.'

'You stop that swearin' now!' Nada turned on Curly in anger. 'Miss Francine is just a very arrogant, bad-tempered lady. I expect she's the same with most folks.'

'Jus' keep out of her way,' Curly warned bluntly.

Within the hour Rosanne was walking up the front steps to find Francine enthroned in the great peacock chair that had come from the Philippines. Marta was seated in the chair beside her and Sharyn was pouring drinks from a tall frosted jug.

'Hello, dear. We were just talking about you.' Marta looked up to smile.

'Hi there.' Francine too flashed a smile, but her hazel eyes were as hard as pebbles. 'How was the ride? Marta's been telling me you've taken to it like a duck to water.'

'How nice to see you.' Rosanne leaned back against the vine-wreathed white pillar, and accepted the cold drink Sharyn passed her. 'I'm gradually getting better and I do so enjoy it. We saw the plane coming in and leaving.'

'*We*?' Francine raised a dark eyebrow.

'Oh, I have an appointed guardian and he's great company.' For some reason, not snobbery, Rosanne didn't want to mention Nada.

'Young Curly,' Marta explained. 'He's a good lad, and Ross doesn't want Rosanne wandering about by herself.'

'Strangely enough I didn't think she'd want to.'

'You don't know her at all,' Sharyn interrupted cheerfully, and gave Rosanne a sidelong smile. 'She's full of surprises. *Nice* ones.'

'Why, thank you!' Rosanne felt a flood of pleasure. From being ultra-touchy Sharyn's manner was improving with her lost inches.

'And you're not worried about having a bad fall?' Francine asked.

'On Lady?' Sharyn's chest heaved. 'Lovely old Lady? Why do you think Ross picked her? He knows she'll carry Rosanne safely.'

'Quite a little champion!' Francine smiled. 'I'd take a good deal of care of myself if I were a dancer.'

'Well, I'd better go and freshen up,' said Rosanne. 'Thanks for the lemonade. It was just what I needed.'

'Give me a little gin in mine!' Francine tilted back her glossy head. 'You really look very brown, Rosanne. Do you think it's wise?'

'Well, for cryin' out loud!' Sharyn stood up and her voice sounded scratchy. 'What are you fussing about, Fran? Rosanne has the best skin I've ever seen and it's the palest gold.'

'Still, for a *dancer*!' Francine shook her head. 'I'm sure Rosanne will agree with me tans are frowned upon.'

'She'll soon lose it,' said Marta, looking a little nervously at her latest guest. 'Ross should be here soon. I hope you're going to make him relax.'

'You're a pet, Marta.' Francine patted the older woman's hand a shade patronisingly. 'Some people thrive on hard work, and Ross is one of them. In fact, he plainly enjoys it. But I'll do my best.'

'See you later.' Rosanne made a little waving motion with her hand. 'I think I'll wash my hair.'

Sharyn grinned at her as if she knew she was making her escape, and it was true she found Francine very heavy weather. As she went back through the house she caught sight of Ross on the walkway and as she stood there hesitating, he looked in and caught sight of her as well.

He didn't call out, but held up his hand gesturing her out, and though her heart trembled she moved out towards him at a leisurely pace. 'I've been wondering when I'd see you.'

'Really?' He threw her an unsettling lazy smile. 'Curly has just been telling me about all your adventures.'

'He's a wonderful guide,' she assured him.

'He is.'

'Nada came with us.'

'I know,' he commented dryly. 'Curly could prove himself a match for any woman talking twenty to the dozen.'

'Francine is here,' Rosanne told him.

'After all, why not?' he looked at her derisively.

'What did you want me for?' It was best to swerve off the subject, especially with his eyes sparkling like that.

'Cleopatra has had her kittens.'

'How clever!' Cleopatra was the kitchen cat.

'Come with me and I'll show you,' he invited.

'Aren't you worried about keeping Francine waiting?'

'It's a long established rule of mine, keeping women waiting.'

'Ah, the reason you're not married.'

'You're getting very sassy, aren't you?' His mouth was touched with the ghost of a smile.

Rosanne walked quickly beside him back towards the stables complex, the moments filled with a dangerous sweetness. Her serenity seemed to fly out the door when he was around. He was so tall, and hard and handsome and so emphatically *male*. It struck her that never in her life had she met a real man before.

'Here we are!' Ross put out his hand and pulled her into one of the quiet stable sheds. 'This one doesn't get as much use as the others, that's why Cleo picked it.'

'I can't see anything.' Rosanne looked around her, trying to adjust her eyes to the dim light.

'You mean to say you can't see *six cats*?'

'Turn the light on and give me a chance.'

'Cleo might resent it. Over here.' He put out his hand again and she had to take it, the tingles running back up her arm. Which was probably exactly what he wanted.

Cleo lifted her head rather weakly, but the kittens were all asleep.

'Friends, Cleo,' Rosanne said softly. 'Friends.'

'I take it you're not a cat-hater?' He looked at her with mocking eyes.

'Why, they're so pretty and neat and they take quite good care of themselves.'

'The trouble is Cleo has too many suitors.'

'I expect you should have found her another name,' she said dryly.

'All right, you've seen them. Let's go.' He lifted her to her feet and looked down into her softened face. 'You missed a lot, didn't you, the way you grew up?'

'Don't feel sorry for me,' she begged.

'Why not let me when I'm in the mood?' he drawled.

'The trouble is you're too changeable.'

'So are you.' He looked at her face, the light gilding of her skin. 'I'll take you out myself tomorrow.'

'That will be ... nice....' she stammered. 'But haven't you forgotten....'

'Francine's here?' He gave a short laugh. 'As a matter of fact I had. I'll take you both out.'

'And do the thing properly.' She couldn't resist the soft jibe and unexpectedly Ross caught at her hair and twined it around his hand. '*Oh!*' she gasped a little, and touched the tip of her tongue to her suddenly dry mouth.

'That's a warning,' he grated.

'I'm really sorry,' she was whispering, shaken by the touch of his hand against her cheek. 'I'd never intentionally provoke you. I know *I'm* the one who's supposed to get all the cracks.'

'But you can make them. That's great!' He pulled her hair gently and she had to lift her face.

'It's getting dark in here,' she said stiffly.

'Nervous?'

'Yes, actually. You know perfectly well you bother me.'

'Okay.' He released her hair. 'But are you sure you know what it is?'

She did, of course, but everything was going too fast. It couldn't *be* anyway, to lose herself with her enemy. She almost rushed away from him saying she had to wash her hair, and a short time later was astounded to find silver buckets of rainwater delivered to her room.

Hours later over dinner Rosanne caught the flicker in Ross's eyes as he glanced at her shining hair. The rainwater had left it like silk and so polished it gleamed under the light from the chandelier.

'You've changed a good deal.' Francine forced her face into a smile. 'It's really great to see you looking so well, you know.'

'Yes, it is!' Marta reached out and touched Rosanne's hand. 'I don't want you to ever leave.'

'Now, now, Marta, she can't stay for ever, you know,' Francine laughed. 'Not if she's to continue her career.'

'I refuse to hear about it now,' Marta said seriously. 'Everything has changed since Rosanne has been here.'

'Hear, hear!' Sharyn glanced at Francine, enjoying her discomfort. 'Even I am far more beautiful than I usually am.'

'Very much slimmer,' Francine smiled.

'Rosanne has given me a series of exercises. I'm enjoying them.'

'Is that what you've been doing in the morning?' her stepbrother glanced at her.

'They're the best,' she assured him.

'Well, I like the result.'

After that, Sharyn bloomed, not needing the slightest encouragement to forgo a slice of a superb apple tart with an apricot glaze. If Rosanne rarely ate sweet things, she could do the same.

The next day Marta wasn't feeling very well, so Rosanne decided to keep her company at the homestead. More for mischief than anything else Sharyn had dressed herself in her riding clothes and announced that she was going to tag along with Francine and Ross.

'You know you hate it, dear,' Francine said rather sharply.

'On the contrary, I can't wait to get back into the saddle,' Sharyn assured her.

'And what is *your* role?' Francine glanced down at Rosanne, who was sitting quietly in a chair. 'Are you sure you're not going to join us?'

'Thank you, no.' Rosanne's answer was mild and friendly, despite the strong undercurrents. 'I'll stay here with Marta.'

'She's taken to you, hasn't she?' From the vibrations in the air Francine might as well have added: How strange!

'I've become fond of her, too.' The only way to play it with Francine was cool, cool, cool.

'Have you any idea when you might have to leave us?'

'Why the concern?' Sharyn asked challengingly.

'Well, Rosanne must keep thinking about it,' Francine offered reasonably. 'After all, dear, she's not a rich girl like you.'

'I think we'd better join Ross.' Sharyn picked up her hat.

'Yes, it's going to be wonderful!' Francine turned back to flash Rosanne a triumphant smile. 'I daresay we'll be out for most of the day.'

Sharyn hesitated and she was scowling again. 'Sure you don't mind staying in, Rosanne? You like riding so much.'

'Of course not,' Rosanne's voice was quiet and calm. 'Marta and I will manage very well.'

'Are you coming, Sharyn?' Francine called to her, 'or are you in two minds?'

'I don't know that I like old Fran,' Sharyn muttered for Rosanne's benefit, 'and I'm sure she thinks there aren't too many minds equal to her own.'

The same idea had got through to Rosanne and she smiled suddenly. 'Go off and enjoy yourself. Also, the more exercise you get, the slimmer you'll get. It's as simple as that!'

'Plain talk, girl. That's what I need.' Sharyn took her leave of her, smiling and undoubtedly very much more attractive on her new régime.

The day passed very peacefully relaxing and having a picnic lunch in the shade of the poincianas, and when Marta retired mid-afternoon for a quiet nap, Rosanne decided she was free to please herself. She knew exactly what she wanted to do; take Lady out to the grasslands or perhaps a little way towards the mountain. It fascinated her. She was confident too, if she kept fairly close to the compound she would have no need of Curly. Though he was good company she had a need to be by herself, and Francine's presence at High Valley had definitely unsettled her. A flicker of some new emotion was there, an emotion she was worried bordered on jealousy.

She had nothing to be jealous about. How absurd! It would be disastrous to fall in love with a man like Ross McAdam even if she had the fear he wanted her to—as a punishment. She couldn't doubt the way his mind worked. Then he could tell her she was exactly the ambitious little opportunist he had despised from the beginning. Robin had done that to her, and she felt no anger towards him. Robin had never come to terms with himself and the anger and suppressed jealousy he felt for his stepbrother had led him to write that final letter. Jealousy had a way of erupting and spilling over, and she had been made to suffer for the jumble in Robin's mind.

Another one of the workers was sweeping the broad paved area in front of the stables and when

he saw Rosanne he leaned on his broom and swept off
his slouch hat.

'Afternoon, miss.'

Rosanne smiled pleasantly and asked automatically
if Curly was around.

'He'll be back in, I'd say, twenty minutes. Why,
miss, d'yah want to take one of the horses out?'

'Lady.'

'Then she's all yours.' The man put his broom
down. I'll saddle her up for yah.'

'Thank you.' It was a good deal easier than she expected. Curly would have undoubtedly argued that she
was ignoring the Boss's orders, and no one did that
around High Valley.

A few minutes later the man led Lady out and gave
Rosanne a leg up into the saddle. 'Goin' anyplace special, miss?' he asked.

'I thought towards the mountain.'

'You're kiddin'!'

'No.' She looked down at the thoughtful chocolate
brown face. 'I'm only going a short way.'

'Maybe you should wait until Curly comes back.'
The man looked less confident.

'I'll be quite all right, really. Lady and I get along
very well.'

The man opened his mouth and closed it again re-
spectfully, and Rosanne took advantage of his hesita-
tion to walk the mare away. There was peace in the
wide, open country and she had so many things to
think about.

Until she had told the man she was going towards
the mountain, she had had no particular destination in
mind; now it seemed to be drawing her. She had
talked with Sharyn about the old abandoned mine up
there, but the rain forest would effectively block her
path.

Thirty minutes later she eased the reins and

turned in the saddle to look back the way she had come. Not very far, actually, and she had enjoyed it immensely. An escape to adventure. Perhaps Ross would let her sleep out under the stars. Her mind went back to the day Curly had told her all about the Sky Country and the great gods that walked the Milky Way. The Aboriginal heritage was no shallow thing but richly imaginative and pervaded with a deep spiritual sense. The gods who lived in the sky as stars had handed down lasting good and wise rules. Both Curly and Nada carried the Dream Life in them, and their intense love of their land and its creatures had to explain the quiet dignity and joy that was in them.

Actually Curly would be upset she had left without him, but there was no need for anxiety on his part. She knew what she was doing. Had she more experience she would have realised she was getting over-confident, but Lady was so gentle, so sweet-tempered and controllable, the impulse to go further was irresistible.

Closer to, Eagle Rock looked huge against the sky. It would be wonderful to climb it, to reach the twin summits that so resembled a great eagle with out-stretched wings. Rosanne remembered Sharyn telling her there was a lot of tin up there. Maybe a mountain of tin. Millions of dollars in one's backyard. It was a rich country.

She had been sitting so long, Lady turned her head back to look at her in her calm, self-possessed way and Rosanne burst out laughing at the mare's expression.

'All right, girl,' she reached down and patted the gleaming chestnut neck, 'we'll go on.'

There were bunches of wildflowers growing every-where beneath the trees and the beautiful little storm flowers that soon died. She knew now that the spirit

of the bush was speaking to her and she started to
sing to herself in a voice just above a whisper. With
a wind catching the words it sounded like a chant
and presently underneath her voice she started to
imagine tap-sticks. The bush was full of magic and
as she took a faint track that led up a slope she saw
away to her right a narrow creek that lay at the foot
of the mountain like a shining silver ribbon.

Large languorous butterflies were flying around
below eye level, magnificent butterflies that lived on
the edge of the tropical rain forests. One settled on
Lady's mane like a welcome, the dazzling blue of the
dragonfly, spreading its wings in the sunlight. There
was so much beauty around her, the air filled with
the scent of the tall flowering trees, she was rapidly
becoming drugged; as drugged as the flocks of honey-
eaters and lorikeets that were attracted to the abun-
dant nectar.

She touched Lady's sides and the mare obediently
took off, shooting away to the right. Being up on a
horse gave Rosanne a feeling of power; a feeling she
had never had before in her life. They were moving
together rhythmically, she and Lady, and she felt
strong and lightheaded all at the same time. Her life
up until now had been like a half empty bucket with
so much to fill her days.

'This looks tricky, Lady!' She shouted to the mare
as they were gaining on the trees and Lady seemed to
check, she thought, then the next thing the mare
stumbled badly and helpless in the face of the unexpected mare and rider took a tumble.

Rosanne had to lie on the ground for a good while
until the air came back into her lungs, then she sat up
breathing deeply. 'Lady!' she called.

The mare was standing a short distance away, very
still and quiet with its right foreleg off the ground.

'Oh, Lady!' She got shakily to her feet and began to dust herself off. 'What have I done to you, girl?'

The mare was making no attempt to put her hoof to the ground and Rosanne thought miserably she had to be in pain. 'If only I knew about horses!' she groaned.

Silently she patted the mare's neck, looking anxiously down at its leg. What was it, a pulled tendon?

'How did we ever get into such a predicament, old girl!'

The answer was a melon hole and checking back Rosanne found it, conscious now that the sun was slipping down the horizon in a splendour of crimson and gold and royal purple. She would have to turn back immediately if she wanted to reach the safety of the compound before twilight. After that, night fell with absolute completeness. No city lights, no street light, just the moon and the stars.

The sight of Lady standing there with her hoof off the ground was upsetting her. Horses, though they looked so splendid and strong, were really delicate creatures. If she had injured Lady badly she would never forgive herself. Neither would Ross. 'We've got to go back, Lady,' she told the horse, but Lady wasn't going anywhere, looking straight down and standing on three legs.

The saddle had to come off and Rosanne unbuckled the girth. Chains of water fowl were passing overhead, assuring her that night was indeed falling. She couldn't ride Lady and she couldn't leave her. Eventually when it was found she hadn't returned, Ross would organise a search party, but could they find her tonight? She began to worry about Curly's fate. Her actions would certainly get him into trouble, the other stable boy as well.

'Why don't I listen, Lady!' she murmured. From

an incredible adventure to the end of the world. But
was it? She wasn't frightened of the dark. She could
camp along the creek bed. If she didn't stumble over
snakes, she thought desperately, they wouldn't worry
her. She looked nervously around her. The bush came
alive at night. All the animal life—fruit and blossom
bats, ugh! possums and wallabies, wild pigs and
donkeys, goannas large as logs foraging the forests and
following the streams.

For all her bravado, her limbs didn't seem to be
functioning properly and she was very glad of the
mare's company. 'Can you hobble, old girl?' she
asked.

The mare countered with an effort that halted
abruptly.

'Oh dear!'

The mare probably knew her own way back to the
compound. Now in the dimming light the landscape
was covered with strange trees. Surely there should
have been a clump of paperbarks? Rosanne moved
closer to the mare's side and sat down. 'He'll find me,'
she whispered. 'He's got to.'

She was still sitting wretchedly when she heard the
first of the 'Cooees!'

The old bushman's call was intensified in the clear
air, carrying through the trees. Her dying hopes fanned
like a fire in the breeze and she jumped to her feet,
cupping her hand around her mouth and imitating the
call.

'Cooee!' Relief made her tremble.

The answering call came again, but she wasn't sure
from which direction. The sky was deep mauve with
grape blue on the horizon and a small tan-red wallaby
suddenly leapt from the grass, stared at her curiously,
then twisted and bounded away towards the creek.

'Oh God, please let him find me!'

She was looking expectantly in the wrong direction, when a horse and rider broke through the trees. Shadows were forming and the boles of the gums had an eerie gleam. She heard the thunder of hooves, a man's cry, and as she spun around with her joined hands to her breast, horse and rider took the savannah in a mighty sweep and reined in hard beside her.

'Don't you *ever* do that again!'

She felt more than saw him dismount and the next minute he was looming over her, so tall and so angry that she felt he, then the sky, were going to fall on top of her.

'I'm sorry!' She couldn't move and the tears started to her eyes.

'Sorry—God!' Ross clamped his hands on her bare arms and almost lifted her off the ground. 'What kind of a fool are you?'

'*Your* kind, apparently!' She heard herself shouting at him, amazed that she could. 'What have I done anyway? I'm not lost.'

'You were going to stay here all night, then?' He gave a jeering laugh and for a moment she thought he was going to forget she was female.

'It's *Lady*, can't you see?' Why was her fright all mixed up with desire?

'I can,' he answered sharply. 'What have you done to her?'

'I *don't know*!' She wailed it because she thought her neck was going to snap.

'Then let's see.' Abruptly he released her and she almost fell against him.

'God, you're a brute!' she muttered.

'What did you expect anyway, *sympathy*?' He strode away to the mare, exuding male arrogance. Incredibly after such a fiery exchange, his voice when he spoke to the injured horse was satiated with the sympathy he wasn't going to waste on a mere woman. 'What is it, old girl?'

'We took a toss.' Nervously Rosanne came to stand at his broad back, watching as he examined the mare.

'I don't believe it!' He glanced back at her jeeringly. 'When I told you you'd make a rider I didn't mean in a couple of days.'

'I was doing fine,' she protested, 'but I'm sorry if I've hurt Lady. Is she all right?' She sank down gloomily beside him. 'Poor old girl, poor Lady.'

'You're not going to cry, are you?' He shoved his Stetson to the back of his head and she could feel the angry heat from his body.

'Yes, I am.'

'For God's sake!' He swore violently under his breath and his eyes slid from her anxious, shimmering eyes, back to the mare's leg. 'Well, forget it. She's pulled a tendon, but otherwise she's O.K.'

'Thank God!' As relief took over, Rosanne sank on to the grass. 'So what do we do now? She won't put her hoof to the ground.'

'Would you, if you were hurting like hell?'

'Gosh, you're nasty!' Like a gazelle, she sprang up and away from him and he gave a sudden burst of laughter.

'Smart move, baby. I was just going to shake you until your teeth rattled. Don't you realise just how worried I've been?'

'*You*, worried about *me*!' She made a wide, dramatic gesture with her arms. 'Please don't make me laugh!'

'I'll guarantee you won't be laughing.' Ross was coming towards her with deadly grace and she took a quick involuntary step backwards.

'Take it easy now!'

'So where are you going to run?'

'You wouldn't!' Her voice sounded badly frightened and the world was getting dark. 'Don't you know how much I hate you?'

'You know damn well you don't!' He was looking down at her, her gold hair and her widened eyes, then suddenly he seemed to relax. 'Let's be friends, little one. There's going to be no one else but the two of us.'

'What do you mean?' She was still clambering away from him, not bothering to turn her head, and she toppled over a hidden root.

'Oh, stop it!' Ross leant over and lifted her to her feet and for some reason his sparkling eyes registered laughter, not anger. 'Or do you think all these silly games are going to turn me on?'

'That's the last thing I'd want to find out!' His fingers were brushing her face and she had to bite on her underlip to prevent a sigh escaping her.

'Which one would I be? Lover number what?'

'No lover—*none*.' Her voice dropped to a whisper and she couldn't look at him.

'Okay, so you don't have to tell me. I know.' He gave a hard, humourless laugh. 'Well, it looks like we're stuck here until morning.'

'You're joking!' Even with the warning her heart turned right over.

'I don't see anything remotely funny about it,' Ross said tersely. 'Lady can't be moved and I'm not going to leave her. We'll camp by the creek and float her back in the morning. What she needs right now is a wet dressing.'

'I'm sorry, I didn't think.' Rosanne flushed hotly, but he didn't even look at her. Instead he vaulted into the saddle of his big bay gelding and put out his hand to her. 'Come on, let's get cracking before the light vanishes.'

She stepped forward quickly, put her foot in the stirrup and gave him her hand and for a second they were thrown together like lovers.

'Oh, gosh!' she exclaimed.

'What's the hurry?' His mouth was near her chin and had she turned her head she would finally have succumbed to something she was craving; to let her mouth touch his skin. But she didn't because she knew he would hurt her.

'All right, I've got you.' His arm slipped around her slight body and he drew her back against him. 'I just hope you didn't do this on purpose, Rosanne.'

She gave an involuntary gasp at his insolence, but he only laughed and sent the gelding on to the creek.

She didn't speak when he lifted her down to the sandy bank, only held her hair away from her face.

'Cat got your tongue?' he asked evenly.

'Silence is golden with some people.'

'No.' He let the gelding drink, then tethered it to a tree. 'If you want to make yourself useful, gather up some firewood. There's plenty around.'

'Another minute and it'll be pitch black,' she protested.

'So what's holding you up? I'll try to get Lady in a bit closer. I might need your shirt for a dressing.'

'What?' She looked up, horrified. She wasn't even wearing a bra.

'Don't you agree she needs one?' he grinned.

'God, you're a tease!' She caught the mocking glint.

'Do you think so? I didn't think dancers found anything embarrassing about displaying their bodies.' He turned away from her, calling to the mare, and Rosanne clicked her tongue and began to quickly pile sticks and fallen twigs together. How had this all happened? To be caught up with him here alone.

Francine would be furious. She might even be out now looking for them.

When Ross came back he merely grunted at her efforts, then bent down and set a match to the twigs and the dry leaves. Immediately the flames sprang to life and she saw the ghost of a smile on his firm mouth. 'I'm sure you've dreamed of sleeping out under the stars.'

'I might be able to cope with someone else but you,' she said wryly.

'Why me?' his eyes flashed to hers, his handsome dark face dangerous. 'Don't you believe you're safe with me?'

'I realise you like playing your own games.'

'So be careful.' He stood up and stripped off his shirt and she sat back, fascinated with the play of firelight on smooth, rippling muscle. She was used to the sight of a man's body, even a male dancer almost naked, yet now the sight of his bare, polished torso made her mouth go dry. She even thought of closing her eyes to break the intensity of her own glance.

Ross didn't concentrate on her at all, but walked to the stream and soaked his shirt in cold water. 'I'll be back in a moment. Poor old Lady needs some attention.'

At least he cared about someone—his horse. Laughter shook her and she felt the least little bit hysterical. It was frightening to meet a man who could wield so much power, to make her feel at last the hot wind of desire. She had led such a sheltered life, protected more by her own fastidiousness than innocence. No one thought anything of sharing a little loving in her own world, but up until now her body had never recognised its master.

Afterwards he made tea for her and made her eat whatever he had, but her flesh burned every time their fingers met. When he spoke to her, she had to force an answer, but she couldn't keep the breathlessness out of her voice. She was acting like a fool, a silly, infatuated schoolgirl, not a young woman who had been looking after herself for a long time.

'Listen, I'm tired!' she finally said determinedly. 'Are you going to show me where I sleep?'

'I really am sorry, I should have told you that right away. You're with me.'

'You're crazy!' she gasped.

'Maybe. I've only got one blanket and I've already given away my shirt.'

'Then I'll lean back against the saddle.'

'We both will. Double park. Listen, baby, before you start yelling, I haven't got seduction on my mind.'

'Who said you had?' Her green eyes were enormous in her small, triangular face.

'It's been on a lot of minds around you. Look at the way that André was acting up.'

'When you were *spying* on us?'

'Watch it, green eyes.' He dragged her to her feet. 'Look at it this way. We could have visitors during the night.'

'So?' Like most women she was full of little terrors —creeping things, crawling things, things with shining eyes across the fire.

'So put all your little fears aside. I'm a man who prides himself on his common sense, and you're a conniving little witch.'

It was hard to keep from hitting him. She wanted to lash out and push him over, but obviously he was too big.

'How did you find me anyway?' She stopped dead and stared at him, a big, handsome man who wasn't even properly dressed.

'I thought you'd never ask. You said something

about losing yourself in this part of the world.' Ross gave her a faint smile and spread out the blanket. 'Come on, blondie, I'm right under control. *So far!*'

'I'm sure the thought of Francine is taking care of that!' Rather rebelliously she curled herself up on the fringed rug.

'Francine is my bosom pal,' he assured her.

'You like your women tall and lean?'

'I wouldn't bother about a ridiculous little thing like you.' He eased off her riding boots and stood up. 'You must admit there's very little of you.'

'Goodnight. You don't mind if I say goodnight?' Rosanne turned her face over on to her hand, hearing her voice had a jarring note.

'Sleep away. And don't worry about anything.'

Lady, it seemed, was always on his mind, for a little while later she saw him return with his shirt, dip it in the stream again, then go back through the trees. Poor old Lady, the only thing they could do for her was keep up the cold dressings.

The fire was burning brightly and there was some heady flower perfume on the air. If she listened she could even hear the plop of small fish in the creek. She settled her head more comfortably and stared up at the stars. They were unutterably lovely, so big and so close she could have put up her hand. No wonder the Aborigines worshipped their heavenly gods. The Southern Cross was easy to pick out, the star furthest to the south, a star of the first magnitude, pointing to the South Pole. Jirrunjoonga, the Guiding One.

The warm silky air gave her a feeling of lightness and luxury and she kept her eyes open for a little while longer. She could escape Ross in sleep, and she had to say she was tired.

Towards midnight, she had her dream again. Being trapped in the car. Turning her head, she could see Robin. She thought he was all right, at first, then she saw the blood.

'*Robin!*' She screamed the name out, one arm jerking wildly above her head. Oh God, he was *dead*!

Steel bands seemed to be clamping her in her place and she knew despairingly she would never get out.

'Help me, *help* me!'

It took Ross some time to bring her out of it and she was sobbing uncontrollably. 'Oh, God!'

'You're safe,' he said quietly.

It was a man who hung over her, a man she knew. His hand was hard against her nape and his eyes were so coldly brilliant the dream faded and harsh reality took its place.

'I was dreaming.' Her voice even sounded as though she had been screaming.

'You're awake now.' He lifted her shaking body into a sitting position. 'You scared the hell out of me, not to speak of the horses.'

'I'd like a drink of water,' she whispered.

'I'll get you one.' He stood up and moved away from her. 'I guess I'm not surprised you have nightmares.'

'What time is it?' She forced herself to breathe deeply. Her dream had been so real she felt raw with pain.

'Oh, about midnight.' He came back to her then, dropping down beside her and offering her the mug of cold water.

'Thank you.' She went to take it from him, but her hand was trembling so much, he took it off her and held it to her mouth.

It was ice-cold and she drank thirstily, like a child. Had she screamed Robin's name aloud? If so, Ross's thoughts would have taken a dark direction.

'How often do you have these dreams?' he asked

bluntly, when she had finished.

'Oh, when I'm tired.'

'How do you feel now?' There was no real concern in the question. More like a hard searching.

'I don't know....' her neck was a little stiff from the way she had been lying. 'I doubt if I'll get back to sleep again.'

'Then it's going to be a long night.'

'So it's not what you want!' she was goaded into replying. 'Why don't you go? I guess you can find your way back easily. I'll look after Lady.'

'Don't scream at me!' He moved her back abruptly so she almost fell on the rug. 'Like you, I'm stuck. It's a long ride back.'

'You really are a brute, aren't you?' she said bitterly.

'You told me that the first time we met.'

Rosanne shook her head, her body stretched taut. This was all a nightmare, spending a night with him. He had turned away from her and his shoulders looked very powerful and wide. Why in hell didn't he have another shirt? As it was, having him beside her had her nerves strung tight.

'Go back to sleep,' he said curtly, and threw a few more sticks on the fire.

'Oh, all right!' Her voice sounded choked and furious. 'And don't you dare lie down beside me without a stitch on your back!'

'That's funny!' He swung on her then and grasped her chin in his hand. 'But you've seen plenty. No, don't widen your eyes at me, so big and so innocent. You have a very sexy mouth.'

She managed a ragged little laugh. 'You're trying to break me, for some reason. *Why?*'

'What's the matter?' he demanded. 'Are you starting to worry that I could?'

'So you can discard me?' She sat up, not caring that she brought herself right up against his hard-muscled body. Her own body was shaking with rage and humiliation.

'What are you out to prove, little one?'

She could see the flare of temper in his silver eyes, but he made no move to touch her.

'That you're a cold-blooded, cynical....'

She got no further, for he set his mouth against hers, bruising her lips and lifting her right into his arms.

'You little bitch!'

She didn't know, didn't care what was happening to her. His assault had rendered her incapable of thought. Only feeling, feeling, the ravishing, punishing. She had never known such demand. The whole world was whirling while he exacted his revenge.

'No fight?' He lifted his head to look down into her face.

She could have flown for him earlier that afternoon, but now? Her mouth parted, wanting to be possessed again even in violence. 'Why not?' his voice seemed to vibrate with contempt. 'You don't shrink from desire, do you? And I desire you—you know that.'

The glitter of his eyes almost brought her to her senses, but as she put out a hand to push at his shoulder he surprised her by bringing her down against the rug, trapping her within his arms.

'To you, dear Rosanne,' he said, and kissed her throat.

'I hate you!' At that moment it seemed true and so very urgent.

'You truly don't!'

She shook her head.

'That's right,' he said idly, 'you don't.'

'Then take pity on me.' She lay still, the soft cloud of her hair fanning out on the plaid rug, her skin gleaming and pearl-like in the dancing light.

'I warned you, girl,' he said mockingly, 'it's going to be a sleepless night.'

'And I swear I'll never forgive you!'

'When it was love at first sight?' He slipped his arms beneath her, arching her body closely against him so her breasts pressed against his naked chest.

Some broken exclamation escaped her, a bitter-sweet terror at the force of discovery, but Ross was kissing her mouth again, not gently, but with a hard, deliberate passion as if he despised himself for not being able to hold back.

Rosanne would never have believed anyone *could* kiss like that. Her heartbeats were shaking her whole body. So much fury, so much passion. Ross slipped his hand to her shirt, opened it and found her breast.

The shock was savage; the maidenly affront and the mind-shattering excitement. 'Oh, *don't!*' she gasped.

He didn't seem to hear her, for his head came down between her breasts and he kissed her, tasting her skin. It was a revelation, the deep founts of sensuality, but when his hands reached her narrow hips she burst into tears.

'Don't weep,' he said in a curious, harsh voice, and touched a hand to her wet cheek.

She tried to speak, but it was impossible. She could only lie there while he stared down urgently into her face.

'You're a strange girl,' he said tightly. 'Do you always weep?'

'I've never lied to you.' Her voice was soft and trembling with emotion.

'Don't start *that* again!' His tone was violent, but

he didn't move, supporting her head in his hands.
'You can't drive a man to craving and then burst into
tears.'

'There's no dignity in the desire you feel for me.'

'I thought you were a girl who sought physical ful-
filment?' His eyes were dazzling in his dark face,
bold and angry.

'I told you, I've never had intimate contact with a
man in my life!' Only you, she thought brokenly.
Only you to break through my defences, a man who
despises me. Wearily she rested her forehead against
his hand, her long silky hair clinging to his wrist, and
he stared at her with a strange twist to his sculptured
mouth.

'I wish to God I could believe you. I'd need to rape
you to find out—and I'm the man who's supposed to
be your protector.'

'I know you are.' His dark face swam in her sight,
but she looked him fully in the eyes.

'There's danger in thinking that, little one,' he said
with faint tenderness. 'I'm a man and an enemy. You
understand?'

'I understand.' She shut her eyes tight in part
ecstasy, part fear. There was a core of fire somewhere
deep in her body, a tumultuous, unsatisfied arousal.
How could she love this man and bring unhappiness
on herself? It was the worst part, the bitterest part of
all, for in too short a time he had invaded and con-
quered her heart. Her mind reeled with the thought
even as her body recognised its master.

She began to weep again for her hopeless passion
and Ross groaned loudly and put her on her side,
just like a baby. 'What a hell of a mess!' He lay down
beside her and threw a strong arm around her waist.
He sounded disillusioned and implacable and she
said tearfully:

'I told you that, remember?'

'Oh, go to sleep. You've got nothing to fear.'

'Don't take your arm away,' she begged vaguely, spent with emotion.

'Sweet God!' There was a touch of humour in his rough, startled tone. 'Sleep, Rosanne, and I'll watch you. I mean, I've got nothing else to do.'

'Don't be angry,' she begged.

Again the short laugh. 'Come back against me, little one, and relax.'

CHAPTER SIX

IN the morning when she opened her eyes, Ross was fast asleep beside her. She brought herself up on her elbows and looked yearningly down into his face.

I love you, she whispered to herself. I love you. I love you. And now you're going to wake up and your eyes will turn to splinters of ice and you'll say things that tear me to pieces.

His skin was so dark, polished bronze. She wanted to touch him, trace the line of his mouth. He had a beautiful mouth—a beautiful, maddening mouth. Free to look at him, she did. His features were strong and emphatic, his shoulders wide, lean powerful torso, the darkly tanned skin matted with hair. He had a scar on his right shoulder, a bad one, that she later discovered had been caused by the rip of a bull's horn.

She wanted to kiss it, but if she kissed him she

would wake him and he would annihilate her with a glance. She didn't know sleep had been impossible for him until almost dawn. Now he lay relaxed, not tough and unbending but accommodatingly hers. She hadn't picked this man to love. It had happened, and she was beyond caring.

A small breeze stirred the leaves and the creek was bathed in a flush of golden light. How beautiful it was, with the birds singing and dipping their jewelled plumage in and out of the trees. They might have been alone in Paradise, only now Rosanne remembered Lady and her green eyes reflected her anxious thought. Stealthily she went to move, only he opened his eyes and it was certain he didn't know her in that first moment, for his eyes were brilliantly clear and in them she saw a strange hunger.

'Hello!' she said softly, her silver-gilt hair falling in a straight curtain on either side of her head.

'Ondine, I presume?' His hand came up and he curled her hair around his palm.

His eyes were still strangely sensual and she gave a little moan she couldn't help. 'I slept like a baby.'

'I know.' His mouth curved.

'How's Lady?' Her heart was fluttering at his glance.

'I'll see to her.' Lithely he came to his feet, drawing her up with him.

'Everyone will be out looking for us.' Close to him, Rosanne felt her frail flesh was dissolving.

'I'm sure you *loved* your night out under the stars?' he drawled mockingly.

'I'll pray there won't be another!' The colour leapt to her cheeks.

'That's going too far.' Ross moved suddenly, so suddenly she was startled, and to her astonishment dropped a hard kiss on her parted mouth. 'I could take poison from your lips, Rosanne.'

'Am I poison?' she asked sadly.

'Not to mention a green-eyed enchantress. You ought to flee me in shame.'

But you would never follow me, she thought with a deep twist of pain.

He was walking away from her with his silent tread, tall and vital, kneeling on a boulder and splashing his face in cold water. The droplets of water glistened in the light and the morning sun lent a silver sheen to his raven hair.

How much she had learnt of herself in one night! Ross had lit a flame in her that would burn for ever. It was a beautiful scene, like an enchanted forest, but when he turned back to her all he said prosaically was :

'I hope to God Harry has the sense to bring a float.'

By mid-morning they were all back at the homestead, including Lady, and Rosanne could tell from Francine's carefully controlled manner that it was only a question of time before Francine sought her out to interrogate her about that shared night. Now it was certain Rosanne hadn't been injured in any way, save for a few bruises and mosquito bites, Marta was all relief and soft gaiety, and Sharyn had looked straight at Rosanne and winked—a definite, conspiratorial wink that gave Rosanne the conviction that Francine alone was perturbed by her 'escapade' —Francine's own word, covering a perturbation that seemed almost too powerful to contain.

Ross had showered and dressed and gone out again, and Rosanne had seen him in the garden with Francine clinging to his arm, obviously pleading with him about something. What was she saying?

Rosanne could only guess. Francine was in her late twenties and Rosanne had seen the agony of jealousy in her eyes. Why hadn't Ross married her before this? Carefully she turned her head away from that sunlit tableau, feeling an ineffable sadness—for herself, for Francine. It was hell to love a man who had only a passing need of women.

A short time later, as Rosanne was tidying up her things, Francine flung open her bedroom door without knocking, aggression in every line of her tall, slim figure.

'Why, Francine?' Rosanne raised her head, startled. What an uncivilised thing to do! She might have been dressing.

'I think you and I had better have a little talk,' said Francine, her eyes ugly.

'About what?' Rosanne tried to feign innocence.

'About why you're here.' Francine strode purposefully into the room. 'The truth is, you're head over heels in love with Ross.'

'No!' Even to her own ears she sounded aghast.

'Aren't you?' Francine laughed grimly. 'I say you *are*.' She came right up to the younger girl and gave her a shove into an armchair. 'There are too many things to give you away.'

'And what has it all got to do with you?' Rosanne countered with some spirit. 'Couldn't we close the door, in any case? I don't want to upset Marta.'

'Oh, no, don't let's upset poor old Marta,' Francine jeered. 'I mean, she's a real cream puff and you don't want to cross her. It's got everything for you, hasn't it, High Valley. After the miserable life you've led.'

Rosanne didn't answer, but got up quietly and shut the door. 'How far are you prepared to go with all your accusations?'

'As far as it takes!' Francine answered bitterly. 'Mother and I could see what you were up to almost immediately, even if Dad was taken in. Any man is worth a try, and Ross is the richest, most dazzling man you've ever seen—a tremendous improvement on poor, neurotic Robin.'

'I know you think I engineered Lady's accident.'

'You bet I do!' Francine glared.

'I didn't,' Rosanne insisted.

'You take Ross off me, and I'll kill you,' Francine said.

'I couldn't!' Rosanne stood quite still, with the seconds stretching away to eternity. 'If he loves you.'

'You bitch!' Francine gave a bitterly humiliated screech, then she almost jumped the distance that separated them and smacked Rosanne across the face. She was appallingly strong and Rosanne's head snapped back. 'Do you really think I'm going to have my life wrecked by a little upstart from nowhere?'

'Get out of here,' said Rosanne, her voice crystal clear.

'I'll ruin you,' Francine said grimly. 'Somehow I'll manage it. Ross is mine—he's always been mine. The one single man I burn for.'

Rosanne got hold of the door knob and tugged the door open. 'Do you always attack people when they get in your way?'

'Something warned me about you right from the beginning.' Jealousy and anger was twisting Francine's confident, good-looking face. 'How can you act so dishonourably?'

'Is that what you believe, or what you want to believe?' Rosanne met the furious glance unwaveringly.

'Tell me then, you *don't* want him!' Francine demanded in a triumphant rage.

'I see no reason why I should answer you at all.' Rosanne gave a delicate little shrug, seemingly immune to Francine's livid fury. 'You wear no ring on your finger, however much you hope fervently. Until then you have no right to ask any other woman questions.'

Francine, goaded, lifted her hand again and Rosanne stared at it indifferently.

'Girls!' Marta had to raise her voice to make herself well and truly heard. 'For God's sake, what's the matter?'

'Are you sure you want to know?' Francine cried mockingly.

Marta's anxiety showed and she dragged a handkerchief out of her pocket and coughed into it in distress.

'Don't upset her.' Rosanne turned to Francine with warning eyes.

'Do you *mind*? Marta has a right to know.'

'*Please*, she's not well.'

Marta walked jerkily towards them and Francine launched into the attack. 'This sly little bitch is making a fool of us all!'

'Oh, no,' protested Marta, clearly no match for Francine.

'You've been terribly wrong about her, Marta, and I'm sorry, but you *have* to know.'

'What is she talking about?' Marta asked Rosanne indistinctly, a whiteness about her mouth.

'She's in a splendid jealous rage, but I wouldn't worry about it,' Rosanne insisted urgently.

'Of course she never loved Robin,' Francine went on.

'What?' Marta turned her head dazedly.

'I said she never loved Robin,' Francine repeated

thickly. 'How could she when she's crazy about Ross?'

'Don't be silly!' Marta made a gesture of disbelief. 'She told me she loved Robin.'

'She lied!' Francine's eyes were a furious blaze. 'I can tell you this, and don't be in any doubt about it, she's after Ross!'

'Francine, Francine,' Marta whispered, and drooped her head.

'I've had about enough. In fact, I've had more than enough!' A flush swept Rosanne's face and she put her arm about Marta's frail shoulders. '*Shut up!* If you're terrified of losing Ross that's your bad luck, but I won't have you disturbing Marta.'

'What impudence!' The furious blood was rising to Francine's high cheekbones and if looks could kill, Rosanne would have been dead on the spot. 'Just wait till I tell Mother!'

'And what's *she* going to do?' At this point, Sharyn's voice intruded and she hurried to her mother's side, patting her shoulder. 'What goes on here?'

'What a scene! What a touching little scene!' Francine's voice rose a little hysterically. 'You've really wormed your way in here!'

'What the hell is she talking about?' Sharyn shouted over Francine's voice.

'Let's take your mother to her room,' Rosanne said urgently.

'Forgive me, Marta,' Francine looked down at Marta's white mute face. 'The last thing I want to do is hurt you, but you have to know. This girl will damage us all.'

'My God!' Sharyn looked at Francine sharply. 'That's a very bad case of jealousy.'

'Don't interfere!' Francine's hand trembled and

shook. 'You all know what I feel for Ross, the plans we've had, my parents' dream. I'm not going to have it all destroyed by this despicable little opportunist. She's seen a new world and now she wants it and she wants Ross.'

'But she loved *Robin*!' Marta pleaded like a broken child. 'She loved my son.'

'Did he ever speak of her love to you?' Francine asked harshly. 'No, we only knew he was going to marry her. He never even had the guts to face you because he knew she was no good.'

'Please, Marta, come away.' Rosanne couldn't stand the sight of Marta's stricken face.

'Tell me she's lying?'

'Yes.' Rosanne, too, was full of a cold desolation. She wished she had never come, never met a man like Ross McAdam. It was quite true what Francine had said. It wasn't wise, or intelligent, but she loved him with her heart's blood.

'I'm going out!' Francine announced, her voice a little hoarse. 'It's always been so wonderful being on High Valley—until now.'

'Then why don't you leave?' Sharyn exclaimed. 'You never come to see *us*, anyway.'

'*Sharyn!*' Marta reproved her daughter. 'How can you speak that way to our guest?'

'I thought as she was yelling the place down I might as well say something.'

'I'm going out. To *Ross*!' said Francine. 'And let me warn you, when I'm mistress of High Valley I won't be as tolerant as he.'

It was a long, uneasy day, but when Ross and Francine walked in together at sundown, Ross was softly whistling and no one could have suspected Francine had ever staged a violent scene in her life. She looked ecstatically happy, her skin shone with health and her eyes gleamed.

'To think he could marry *her*!' Sharyn whispered 'Maybe he's even asked her, the way she looks.'

Rosanne even steeled herself to hear an announcement over dinner, but although Francine positively scintillated, especially since the others were so quiet, nothing world-shattering was said. She was off in the morning, in any case, to attend the three-day Central Queensland Brahman stud bull auction with Ross and her spirits were very high.

Much later that night Rosanne stood beside Marta's bed, looking down at her sweet, appealing face.

'Sure you're feeling better?' she asked.

'Yes, dear.' Marta smiled at her. 'Be a good girl and send Sharyn to me, will you? You've made me aware I've been neglecting her and why. My mind was obsessed with my son's death and I became remote from my daughters. Julie can manage, she's self-sufficient and she has Jake, but Sharyn has suffered—I see that now.'

'She loves you,' Rosanne answered. 'I do too.'

'Ah, child.' Marta lifted her dark eyes and stared into Rosanne's face. 'If only Robin had brought you to High Valley at the beginning! You did love him, didn't you?'

'I was going to marry him.' Rosanne's voice was shaking and a bright shimmer came over Marta's eyes.

'Forgive me, dear. I know it's hard to remember, but your memories were sweet.'

'God bless!' Rosanne bent her head and kissed the soft cheek. 'I'll send Sharyn up.'

'I do know you've done wonders together,' Marta said more happily. 'She's really regaining her petite figure. I had a figure like that as a young bride.'

'You still have!' Rosanne turned back to smile at her.

'When the sale is over, we're going to have a few people in to meet you,' Marta decided. 'Not a large crowd, about a hundred or so.'

'Please, Marta, don't go to the bother.' Rosanne was startled and not really pleased.

'No bother at all!' Marta drew a deep, relaxed breath. 'You girls can help me. Julie is a marvel when it comes to organising and a young man you've heard about called Brad Parker is just about due back home. He's been in the States on a study tour. Sharyn will be pleased, I know, to find some excuse to get him here.'

'You're too kind.'

'Kind? No,' said Marta. 'I'm just coming out of the darkness of a long tunnel and I want to share it with you. You're a good girl, Rosanne, such a good girl. I don't want you ever to leave.'

It was very quiet downstairs and Rosanne found Sharyn out on the verandah. 'Your mother wants you,' she told her.

'Oh, good!' Sharyn swung round with a smile. 'She never really forgot about me, you know.'

'Of course she didn't!' Rosanne agreed with certainty. 'She's just been telling me in fact how she's going to give a party so you can invite a certain Brad.'

'Oh, beauty!' Sharyn gave a startled cry of joy. 'I'll have to get a new dress. Nothing I've got will fit me any more, thank God. You'll have to get one too. Not that you don't look pretty in everything, but you must have something grand. Oh, I'm so *happy*!' Sharyn ran from her, with a young girl's exultant face, leaving Rosanne to look out over the garden. She couldn't tolerate the thought of seeing Francine again, so she decided she had better take refuge in her room.

Sharyn had got into the habit of coming in to chat before bed, and until then she could read or write a few letters.

Francine seemed to have forgotten the violently distasteful scene of the morning, so it was easy to assume Ross had made love to her as he must have made love to dozens of willing women. After all, he wasn't a boy, but a handsome and worldly man in his early thirties. Theirs would be a perfect match anyway, both landed gentry, both of them cruel.

In the scented darkness Rosanne felt the touch of his lips on her mouth, the fevered passion, that had haunted her day long. She didn't see at first a man and woman wander around the side of the house from the direction of the staff bungalows, but when she did she shrank back. Ross McAdam could marry anyone he liked. A penniless, inexperienced little dancer would be helpless to cope with him.

In the morning Ross sought her out before breakfast, crossing the lawn to where she sat on a stone bench waiting for the peacocks to stroll along.

'Rosanne?'

She wanted to hide from him, dive into the shrubs, anything but stay there and let him drain all her strength from her.

'Are you planning on avoiding me?' he demanded.

'All I'm doing is sitting here quietly waiting for the peacocks.'

'Prickly little cactus!'

'Sorry.' She turned and gave him a charming, false smile. 'Good morning, Mr McAdam.'

'Want to come to Rocky?'

'With you?' Her voice almost cracked in surprise. 'Aren't you taking your fiancée-to-be?'

'So does that stop me from taking anyone else?'

'You're a cool one, aren't you?' Lights flashed in

her green eyes. 'Forget it, Ross, Just forget it. Your Francine doesn't like me.'

'You can't win 'em all,' he said soothingly. 'I thought you might like to see the big sale. I'm planning on buying and there's plenty else to entertain you.'

'I think I'd better stay here with Marta,' she told him.

'Honestly she won't mind.' He slanted a look down at her slightly withdrawn face. Her silvery fair hair was blowing in the breeze and he let his glance slip to her supple, slender body. 'Besides, you could do with a few clothes. I'm getting kind of sick of seeing you in the same old things.'

'Are we still arguing about that?' She looked up at him with sudden heat. 'I never said I wanted you to admire me.'

'Another minute and I'll turn you over my knee!' he warned.

'Don't say it as though you'd enjoy it.'

'It adds a little excitement,' he agreed. 'Well, are you coming? I want to get away about ten.'

Out of the corner of her eye she saw Francine come out on to the verandah, lean on the white cast-iron railing and finally look their way. 'You're an insensitive brute, aren't you?'

'You'll soon get used to it.' He turned and looked in the direction of her glance. 'Weren't you used to jealousy in the ballet? Your friend Danielle told me you used to make things pretty tense.'

'Danielle always was and always will be an appalling liar.'

'Of course you'd have to say that.' He gave her a flat measuring look from his silver eyes. 'Didn't it bother you that you collected so many of the other girls' boy-friends?'

'Stop it! You're talking makebelieve. My whole life has been *work*.'

'Then you won't mind if I intend keeping you around?'

'I don't want to come, Ross,' she said jerkily. 'Surely you understand.'

'Then I'll go shopping for you,' he said curtly. 'If Marta's planning on having you meet people, you're not going to look like an impassioned little waif.'

'Go to hell!' Just saying it gave her tremendous relief.

'Forget the cheek.' He reached out and trapped her wrist. 'Just behave yourself while I'm gone. Curly will stick to you like glue, I give you my word. With Lady out of action you'll be safe on Idle.'

'Great! That sounds like a rocking horse.'

'Come on, let's go in to breakfast, shall we?' In full view of Francine Ross tucked her arm under his. 'If you don't push it, one of these days I'll find you a good horse of your own.'

Over the next couple of days, Rosanne and Marta drew closer together. Sharyn, when she had heard Rosanne was quite content to stay home, had jumped at the chance of doing a little shopping. Now that she had shed weight and established a beauty routine, no thought pleased her better than shopping for new make-up and clothes, and she planned on having her hair styled as well. It was good hair like her mother's, but it needed expert shaping. She had been all smiles on the morning they departed and Rosanne couldn't help thinking it would be pretty good at that not to have to worry about money.

Two days went past, very quiet, very comfortable; an unruffled delight for Marta and a period of respite for Rosanne. Marta spoke about many things, seemingly going back to the time when she was an eager, frightened bride. She had never felt secure and Rosanne supposed she never would. It must have been a torture to know the husband she loved had never ceased to love his first wife. Yet Marta spoke naturally and easily, not appearing to mind that she was giving Rosanne a deep insight into her private life. In fact, having Rosanne as a confidante appeared to be giving her peace. Rosanne was a good listener with a deep sensitivity and Marta knew intuitively that all the old secrets were safe.

As usual, Rosanne continued with her practising. It was vital to keep her body in shape. One day soon she would be returning to her own world. The world she had once adored, now the thought of it depressed her a little. How odd! Late that afternoon, with some Debussy playing, she worked until she ached. No other life was possible for her, so she had to concentrate on exactly what she had. *All* she had; a talent other dancers seemed to envy.

In her black leotard with her pale golden hair dragged ruthlessly into a knot, she whirled around the room in her pink pointe shoes, oblivious of the young man who had sauntered towards the room, drawn by the music, then remained as her audience.

Finally, when Rosanne stopped, he came away from the door jamb, swaggered into the room and put his hands together in a slow, half admiring, half mocking clap.

'That was *terrific*!'

Still faintly dizzy from a beautiful chain of pirouettes, she turned to him, frowning. 'Where did you come from?'

'At least a thousand miles away.' His black eyes flashed over her face and body as though it was a real pleasure. 'Dale Curtis, the housekeeper's prodigal son.'

'Oh, how are you?' She picked up her long robe

and elbowed into it. 'I'm Rosanne—Rosanne Grey.'

'I can't remember dear Robin ever dating a girl like you.' His words were disturbing; even more, the expression in his eyes.

'Have you come to see your mother?' Not quite understanding her disquiet, Rosanne reached up and pulled the tight rubber band from her hair.

'It's not often these days I can manage it.' His black eyes followed the rippling slide of her hair. 'It pays to come when the master's not at home.'

'He'll be home tomorrow,' Rosanne said as though the thought alone stopped her from panicking. There was something about this young man she disliked, though he was good-looking in a gypsyish sort of way. He was wearing very tight blue jeans and a T-shirt and his black curly hair tumbled forward on his forehead.

'And what do you think of him, the all-powerful, almighty McAdam?'

'You seem to forget Mr McAdam is my host.'

He laughed contemptuously, but a little colour flooded his swarthy skin. 'That's right, doll, put me in my place.'

'That wasn't my intention,' she said coolly, but it was.

'If it's not a sacrilege to speak against the dead, your Robin hated his stepbrother's guts.'

'He did not, he *loved* him!'

'No, girl. I saw him with my own eyes. You ought to have been here. Poor old Robin made his own hell. He didn't come up to the McAdam standard and it ate into him until he was mad with it. Ross had all the courage and brains while Robin never even cared about horses.'

'Then you must have known how he was suffering,' Rosanne challenged him with her head up. 'I don't know about Robin on his home ground, but I saw the best of him. He was sweet and considerate and great fun.'

'And you were going to marry him,' he jeered. 'You would never have married him had he brought you home.'

'I can't think what you mean,' she said sharply.

'Ah, forget it, let's be friends.' Dale Curtis put out his hand and Rosanne very nearly recoiled. Instinct told her he could be callous and over-sexed. Something about her seemed to be exciting him, and as he came at her she walked away and switched off the music.

'Have you seen Mrs McAdam?' she asked him.

'No, I haven't,' he said flatly, and dropped his hand. 'She's asleep. Sleeps her life away, does Marta. I suppose you know after Sharyn her husband never came to her bed.'

'How dare you!' Rosanne felt almost cold and very sick.

'I do dare. I can't help it.' His eyes wandered down her satin robe. 'I wonder Robin had the sense to pick on you.'

'You must excuse me.' Rosanne looked away from him and picked up her things. 'You ought not to have come here, feeling the way you do.'

'Girlie, I'm broke. I mean really broke.'

'And your mother helps you out?'

'I hate little blonde dollies looking me up and down as though I was a prize creep,' he observed.

'I'm sorry, I don't mean to be rude.' She had no alternative but to go past him if she wanted to reach the door.

'You're dynamite when you dance,' he said suddenly. 'One hell of a beautiful little body. Your face isn't bad either. Big green eyes saying, *leave me alone!*

'Get out of the way!' He was blocking her path to the door.

'Say *please*.'

'Okay—*Please*.'

'I'll just bet McAdam fancies you,' he drawled.

Her voice was icy with contempt. 'As you've been around so long you ought to know where his fancy lies.'

'Stupid!' He reached out and touched her flushed face. 'You're not talking about Miss Bitchy Stuck-Up Grant-Taylor? Because he's definitely not going to marry her. I know *him*.'

'Then you must know he'd be very angry to see you blocking my way.'

At that, his eyes changed and he stepped back. 'I'm only having a bit of fun.'

Rosanne went past him quickly to the arched doorway and as she reached it, Mrs Curtis was coming down the wide passageway. There were spots of unaccustomed colour on her high cheekbones and her dark eyes were searching.

'Good evening, miss.'

'Good evening.' Rosanne smiled but it felt a little tight.

'Ah, here's Mamma!' Dale Curtis came into sight, exclaiming in a derisive, high-pitched tone. 'I've just been making Miss Grey's acquaintance.'

'Is everything all right, miss?' Mrs Curtis's somewhat harsh face suddenly looked old and anxious.

'Of course.' Rosanne tried to do a little better with her fixed smile. 'Excuse me, please, I'm standing in a draught.'

Mercifully Dale wasn't invited to the dinner table, but on the two occasions Mrs Curtis appeared,

Rosanne was conscious of the strain behind her
sternly controlled face. Dale was probably a mon-
strous son and a drain on his mother's financial re-
sources. Later that night she thought she saw him
standing in the garden looking up at her room and
she found herself praying for Ross's return. Not that
they were alone. There were plenty of trusted men
on the property, but Dale Curtis worried her, and she
hated his smile.

The next day wore on, Rosanne had decided not
to go riding even with Curly to watch her and mid-
afternoon the Golden Eagle flew in. She saw it before she heard it, and it seemed like her passport to
freedom. With Ross home, she had nothing to fear
from the station's latest, unexpected arrival. She
would be able to take Idle out for a time and be back
when everyone had settled in. Francine wouldn't
want her in the welcoming party anway.

Down at the stables Curly had gone, but with a
somewhat reckless, triumphant air Rosanne saddled
up the grey gelding herself. Curly couldn't possibly
get into trouble. She had told him emphatically she
didn't intend riding that day, though naturally she
had to hide her reason for not wanting to from him.
She wasn't going anywhere in any case and the
chance of being out in the open she wasn't going to
pass up.

Twenty minutes later, with her uneasy feelings
lifted from her, she turned the quiet gelding along the
grassy track that led back to the main compound.

'That was a nice ride, wasn't it?' She had formed
the habit of talking to the horses and Idle's ears
twitched back, sensitive to her every word. It was a
beautiful afternoon, the sun dazzling through the
trees, and she let her cream slouch hat that Sharyn
had given her hang down her back by its strap. How

tragic that Robin had been born with a fear of horses. The love of them should have been in his blood, yet he had developed a bad allergy, so he wouldn't have to come in contact with them. There was still so much about Robin she didn't know.

When she reached the first line of fences, a man was standing so still in the shadow of the trees she didn't see him at first. Then she recognised the stance of the slim, compact body, then the face shaded by a battered old ten-gallon.

'Howdy!' he said gently. He opened the gate for her and the gelding went quietly in.

'I thought I saw the plane arrive,' she said.

'And if you did?'

'I'd best get on home and say hello.'

'Nothing will happen if you stay.' Dale's upward gaze was bright and still.

'I don't want to.'

'Are you sure you know what you want, little girl?' He suddenly smiled and went to stand at the gelding's head holding on to the reins.

'What exactly is your interest in me?' Rosanne asked sharply.

'Don't look so worried. I'm not likely to hurt you.' His voice sounded menacing now and just when she went to spur the horse into action he suddenly gripped her around the waist and almost ripped her from the saddle.

She was so shocked she couldn't scream, and he grabbed a handful of her hair and yanked her face back. 'Know something? I haven't stopped thinking about you.'

'You've stopped thinking, *period*!' she hissed painfully. It was unbelievable she had found herself in this situation with a complete stranger.

'Blondes always have a special magic. Especially

big-eyed, soft-looking blondes.'

'I want you to know I'm going to report this!' she snapped.

'What the hell do you mean? I haven't touched you.' He started to laugh and it bothered her dreadfully. He was obviously a creature of impulse, cunning in one way, yet stupidly unpredictable. 'Why don't you tell me what you saw in Robin? I hadn't seen him in ages, but I do know he had lots of problems.'

'Yes, all right.' The best thing she could do was humour him, then when she got the opportunity run for her life.

'Come on, then.' Dale laughed aloud again. 'Let's go over there and sit down.'

'Hadn't you better tether Idle?' she queried.

'What?' He looked at her questioningly, but she smiled silkily and moved off a little way towards a magnificent, spreading shade tree. 'You can handle a lot of men, can't you, baby?' he said admiringly.

Not even one. She wanted to scream it, but there wasn't time. Dale was walking the gelding, stupidly confident, and she cringed inside at the thought that if she ran he would swing into the saddle and ride her down. What a nightmare, but she had to do something.

Now with his back to her she took off on winged feet with no clear idea of where she was heading, past caring. Any direction she took would bring help. She didn't enjoy being frightened.

Naturally fleet of foot, she vaulted over prop roots, dodged vines, expecting every minute to hear the heavy drum of hooves. The grounds had never seemed so enormous, so heavily wooded, but there up ahead was the outline of a huge shed.

Her mad flight lasted only a few seconds more, for

hard hands descended on her and almost snatched her off her feet.

'What's happening?'

It was Ross's face above her and she was too winded to tell him.

'*Rosanne?*' His frown was ferocious, yet she was never so pleased to see a frown in her life.

'Why are you running?'

She was trembling so much with relief she was all but slumped against him. Abruptly he shifted his gaze from her pale, distraught face and let it range over the trees. 'Is it Curtis?' he flung out the name in contempt.

'No, no.' She knew better than to say yes. He looked violently angry, a big man of superior height and weight to the somehow pathetic Dale.

'Stay here.' His silver eyes burned over her like ice, then he was moving off in the direction from whence Rosanne had run.

Without his support, she just folded up in the grass, almost dazed with relief. A little later a sound like a human cry made her start, but then there was a long silence. She took a deep breath, glanced back through the trees and got shakily to her feet. An extra button on her shirt had come undone and you could see the shadowed cleft of her breast. She went to fix it, then discovered the button had gone.

'Oh, damn!' she said in disgust.

When she turned her head again, Ross was riding the grey gelding, his handsome head high, the lean body very straight. Even at a distance she could tell he was still violently angry. She stood rooted to the spot, her eyes mesmerically following him, then he was beside her, Idle whinneying with pleasure.

'It's a while before you'll be seeing Curtis again,' he told her.

'I certainly hope so.' She looked up at him warily.

'I thought I told you about not going out unaccompanied?'

'I know,' she spoke placatingly, 'but I do so love to ride.'

'*Ride*, indeed!' He looked her over with a hard, alert face. 'Curtis told me you wanted his company.'

'Do you *mind*!' She thought again of her instant distaste and her eyes went huge with indignation.

'As a matter of fact, I do!' he said bluntly. 'A woman would have to be out of her mind to encourage that moron.'

'And I'm *that* stupid?' She stamped her foot.

'Evidently you get a lot of practice.'

'You devil!' A wild tremor shot through her. 'Here I've been praying you'd rescue me and that's all you can say?'

'See here,' he said, and dismounted, 'I told you to stay put.'

'I'm not a child,' as he advanced towards her, she retreated. 'Why can't you remember it?'

'What's all this about?' He put a hand to her unbuttoned shirt, and he sounded deadly earnest and dangerously quiet.

'So the button fell off!' She had a tiny, velvety mole near her left breast.

'Did he touch you?' he asked briefly.

'No.' She caught at his steel wrist. 'Please, Ross, let's forget it.'

'My dear girl, whatever happens here is *my* business.'

'But damn it all, nothing happened.' She stared up at him, her green eyes enormous. 'I always run anyway. It's safer.' Her hand, unknown to her, was clutching convulsively at his. He looked so tough and dangerous she had to tread very carefully.

'So he got the idea first?' His eyes glittered over her, bright as diamonds.

'Ross.' Her voice broken on his name. 'Why do you make me out something I'm not?' She shuddered and suddenly felt like crying. To be thought a siren was driving her mad—she who had been a model of virtue all her life. In some agitation she lifted her hands and pressed them against her temples. 'I want to go home, back to my own life, I'll never bother you again!'

'Hush!' He suddenly cradled her in his arms. 'Be still for a moment.'

overwrought to be comforted.

'I think you're making yourself suffer.'

'What?' At the odd note in his voice she lifted her head.

'You heard.' He looked at her through heavy-lidded eyes.

'I've missed you.' The mad urge possessed her to tell him.

'That's it, little one,' he drawled, 'live up to your image.'

'Damn!' She swore beneath her breath. It would always be there, the accusation, but as she tried to pull away from him, his hands tightened around her rib cage.

'How can good come out of bad? Tell me.'

'I've never done anything bad in my life, but why am I wasting time talking?'

'You're so right!' Like a renewed punishment he covered her mouth savagely, sweeping her into such a hard embrace, she moaned. Then in spite of everything, the deliberate cruelty, her willowy body relaxed, moved against him, and she opened her mouth so he would explore it more fully. Whatever demands he made on her, he was so perfectly, physically acceptable to her she couldn't imagine ever in her life responding the same way to another man. She had told herself she loved him, but telling *him* was something else again.

'For God's sake!' he released her and shook his head, his eyes startling in his dark face.

Like a puppet Rosanne was down on the ground again, only this time the earth seemed to be rocking crazily. Why did she keep throwing herself at him this way? It was so shockingly out of character. 'Can I go now?' she whispered.

'Listen, darling, you've got no equal!' Ross said it as though it was some kind of curse.

'*Stop it!*' This time she did burst into tears, putting her hands to her flushed creamy skin. 'Stop it, stop it! I only wish you'd leave me alone.'

'*Amen!*' He suddenly got hold of her and thrust her up into the saddle. 'Go on home before you get what you're asking for.'

CHAPTER SEVEN

SHARYN came back laden down with presents; a state of affairs that plainly outraged Francine, for a good many of them were for Rosanne.

Lifting dress after dress up in her bedroom, Rosanne felt stupefied by so much extravagance.

'But *Sharyn!*' Her voice broke suspiciously.

'All for you,' Sharyn soothed her. 'What else do

you do with money if you don't spend it?'

'But I can't accept all this!' Rosanne looked help-
lessly around the room. There were clothes everywhere, beautiful things—day dresses, evening wear,
night clothes, the jeans and small shirts she lived in,
but of much better quality, the shirts embroidered
on the pockets, a beautiful pair of jodhpurs, shiny
riding boots, shoes from the best boutiques. There
was even make-up by Orlane and French perfume.

'But you *can*!' Sharyn was laughing and excited.
She had bought almost as much for herself again.
'You're a woman, no exception to the rule. We all
love beautiful things.'

'But few of us have a million dollars.'

'Ross wanted you to have them,' Sharyn said as
though it settled it. 'It was no trouble coming up with
your size, and I pinched a pair of your shoes.'

'Oh, dear!' Rosanne picked up a filmy nightdress
and held it to her face.

'What's the matter?' Sharyn asked in a sudden
panic, seeing nothing of Rosanne but her shining
blonde hair.

'I'm not used to such ... goodness.'

'I think you deserve it.' Sharyn pulled the nightgown away and searched Rosanne's face. 'You
haven't told me what you thought of my hairstyle.'

'I have. You're looking great.'

'Then just remember who set me on the right path.'
Sharyn turned around to study her attractive reflection. 'I haven't felt this good in a long time.'

'Enter Brad Parker,' said Rosanne, and managed
a laugh.

'It's about time I found myself a lover,' Sharyn said
playfully. 'They say it makes a woman bloom. By
the way,' she released the stopper on Rosanne's new
French perfume and touched some of it to her wrists,

'Mother wants to see some of your new clothes. Mine too. We'll make it a parade.'

'As long as no one else wants to see them,' said Rosanne, remembering Francine's face, but Sharyn had whisked away to the door. 'Choose what you like, but don't let anyone see your party dress. That's going to be a secret.'

To Rosanne's consternation Ross was in the drawing room instead of his study. Francine, too, was there, smiling rigidly as the girls showed off their new clothes.

'You *are* a lucky girl, Rosanne!' she commented frequently.

'Why not?' Marta smiled. 'I see it as her right.'

'What do you say, Ross?' Francine asked.

'Cute. Definitely cute.' He finished his whisky and water and pushed the glass away. Both girls were wearing silk 'easy' clothes, Rosanne's with a delicate camisole top that made the most of her small, graceful figure, Sharyn's with a wrapover sleeveless top.

'I mean, all this *expense*!' Francine re-crossed her long, slender legs.

'Which is one hell of a jarring note,' he said calmly. 'How much *was* it?'

'You spend a darn sight more on those stud bulls,' Sharyn gave another twirl.

'I can't thank you enough.' Over Marta's fluffy head Rosanne met a pair of sparkling, mocking eyes.

'I'll find some way,' he returned lightly. 'Now if the parade's over, I'm going over to see Bob. There's been a terrific upswing in the stud market.'

'Do you mind if I tag along?' Francine came rather jerkily to her feet, fixing Ross with pleading hazel eyes. 'Dad is certain to ask me how everything went.'

'Then come along,' he smiled at her. 'You understand the market better than most women.'

'Bully!' said Sharyn, after they were gone. 'Fran is forcing the pace a bit, isn't she?'

'I feel sorry for her,' Rosanne said softly, speaking her thoughts aloud.

'Oh, why?' Sharyn stared at her open-mouthed.

'It would be difficult to reach Ross.'

'I know what you mean,' Marta agreed softly, and there were long years of sadness in her gentle dark eyes.

Rosanne was just about to clamber into bed when some sixth instinct made her turn her head.

She screamed and the instant the cry died away, screamed again. A current of perfumed night air blew in her face and the insect screen she closed if she didn't want to pull her net was wide open.

'Oh, *God*!' She stood up in the middle of the huge, canopied bed, shivering in her thin nightdress, transfixed by an indescribable terror.

A snake was lying indolently half in and half out of her room, a dark snake, olive green or black with funny criss-cross markings along its length. It wasn't very long, probably not four feet, but she knew with the same strange instinct that it was no ordinary garden snake.

She didn't hear the loud murmur of voices, nor did she turn her head when her bedroom door was flung open and Ross strode in. 'My God, not another nightmare?'

The light was raying through her nightdress, turning it almost transparent, but she was aware of nothing; she was on the verge of passing out.

'*Rosanne?*' He got hold of her swept her off her feet so she had to lie on the bed.

'A *snake*!' A board creaked and she almost screamed again.

'Where?' He swung about, strange shadows on his face.

'On the balcony.' Sweat was breaking out all over her body and she rolled about and hid her face in the bedclothes.

'What's wrong?' Sharyn's voice was asking sharply from somewhere beyond her.

'Get back!' That was Ross's voice, loaded with authority.

'Well, I never!' Sharyn's voice rose to a shriek. 'Ross, be careful!'

Rosanne tried to turn over, but she couldn't. She was almost rigid with revulsion, so when Sharyn touched her, she nearly jumped out of her skin.

'I'm sorry, Rose,' Sharyn's golden skin had turned paper-white. 'It's all right, now. Really it is.'

'Are you sure? I hate snakes.'

'I'm afraid of them myself, but most of them are shy of people.'

'They should be.' Rosanne turned over and sat up shakily. 'Where's Ross?'

'I think he's getting you a brandy.' Sharyn sank on the bed and when it protested she giggled weakly. 'I hope he gets one for me!'

'Where's the snake?' With a great effort, Rosanne turned her head over her shoulder.

'Ross killed it.'

'How?' Rosanne's green eyes were dominating her face.

'Dashed its brains out.'

'Oh, yuck!'

'You did ask,' Sharyn pointed out.

'How did it get here?'

'Now that part of it's decidedly odd.' Sharyn was

fiddling with her robe, her eyes narrowed. 'I couldn't tell you when I last saw a tiger snake, and we very rarely have a snake get into the house.'

'Are you suggesting someone put it there?' Rosanne asked weakly.

'They'd be uncommonly brave or they knew how to handle snakes. Ross just picked the damned thing up.'

'He wouldn't!' Rosanne was truly shocked.

'Why wasn't your insect screen shut?' asked Sharyn.

'I thought it was, then something made me turn my head.' Rosanne began to shiver, and Sharyn looked up in relief as her stepbrother strode back into the room.

'Here, drink this.' He passed her a crystal tumbler with about an inch of cognac in it.

'I don't think so,' she protested.

'*Drink* it.' He meant it.

'Yes, sir!' she said flatly.

Sharyn's dark eyes brooded on his. 'How the devil did it get on to the balcony?' she asked.

'You never know. We'll drop it for the moment, Sharyn,' he said with decision.

'Was that necessary?' Rosanne seemed to be offended with the taste of the finest French brandy.

'It will pull you together fairly quickly.' Ross took the glass out of her hand. 'Marta heard your screams, but I told her you had a nightmare.'

'I'd better go to her.' Sharyn fairly jumped off the bed. 'Are you sure you're all right now?' She looked earnestly into Rosanne's dazed face.

'I'll look after her,' Ross said levelly. 'Don't tell your mother about the snake, it would only upset her.'

'What shall I say then?' Sharyn cleared her throat.

'There was something quite....'

'Of course,' Ross agreed emphatically, chopping her off. 'Just say what I said. Rosanne had a nightmare but she's perfectly all right now.'

'All right,' Sharyn sighed. 'As I see it, there's been a bit of skulduggery.'

'Goodnight, Sharyn,' said Ross.

'Very well.' Sharyn gave a little grimace. 'Goodnight, Rosanne. Try not to think about it. It will never happen again.'

There was quite a long pause after she had gone, and Rosanne lay there, thinking cognac was subtle stuff. The worst of her tremors were over and she was ready to remember that though her nightgown was beautiful it plunged deeply and was only shadows away from being transparent.

'I can't sleep here,' she said finally.

'Make a clean start with me.' Ross's tone was dry.

'I'm frightened—don't you see that? That snake.'

'So what do you want me to do, hold you all night?' He caught her eyes and gave a faintly wry smile.

'I don't want anything really terrible to happen.'

'It's going to happen some time!' He slanted a look from her face down the length of her body. 'That's a beautiful nightgown. What there is of it.'

'How can I dream of nice things when you look at me like that?' she demanded.

'Why don't you tell me, which way is that?'

'Dare I break up this cosy little scene?' a glacial voice said from the door.

'Ah, Fran!' Ross turned and stood up, though his voice was quite calm. 'Where have you been all this time?'

Rosanne reached for her robe and slipped her arms into it. 'I think I'll go downstairs if it's not too much trouble and have a cup of tea.'

'*Please!* Would someone mind telling me what this is all about?' Francine looked down her straight nose. She was wearing an exquisite vibrant blue kimono over her nightgown, but Rosanne noticed immediately that she hadn't taken her make-up off.

'There was a snake in my room,' Rosanne explained, and shuddered. 'A tiger snake.'

'What nonsense!' Francine looked coldly contemptuous.

'Not nonsense,' Ross shrugged. 'Not at all.'

'I don't believe it!' Colour flamed into Francine's face and her eyes looked glazed. 'You really *saw* it, Ross?'

'Hell, I killed the damn thing.'

'I really am going to have a cup of tea!' said Rosanne, very small and slight at his side.

'You're all right?' Ross turned his head swiftly to look at her.

'Yes!' Her answer seemed to wobble.

'How she *loves* attention!' Francine cried.

Ross's handsome dark face gave nothing away, yet he turned and lifted Rosanne off her feet. 'What about if I carry you downstairs?'

'Dash it, Ross, she can walk!' protested Francine.

'I don't believe she can.'

'You're making too much of her. You *all* are!' Francine maintained with the utmost virulence.

'Now that's downright unfair,' Ross told her crisply. 'The McAdams are known to be cordial, hospitable people.

'It's all right, Ross,' Rosanne said more firmly. 'Put me down.'

'You might as well. She's only pretending to be

frightened!' Francine laughed incredulously. 'I'm surprised at you, Ross.'

'There are a few things about you that surprise me too.' He fixed his light eyes on her and Francine flushed violently.

'Look here, you're not blaming *me* for anything that happened tonight?'

'Of course he isn't!' Rosanne threw up her arms and just as she had done once before made a balletic leap out of Ross's arms.

'Look, you've got to teach me that trick,' he said laconically. 'It's demoralising to have a woman get away from me so easily.'

'I say, she's dangerous!' A bright colour burned in Francine's face. 'Have you forgotten how she made Robin suffer?'

'That's why you hate her?' Ross asked gently.

'You're horrible, Ross!' Francine cried. 'I don't know why I came.'

Rosanne glanced away, distressed on her account, and Francine wheeled abruptly and raced back along the gallery to her room.

'You've hurt her,' she told Ross quietly.

'I believe I have.'

She fixed her green eyes on him accusingly. 'I wouldn't want to be the woman to marry you. You're ruthless!'

'Don't get excited.' He was looking gravely into her eyes without even seeing her. 'Are you sure you don't want to sleep here?'

'Do you think a snake could get up on to the balcony like that?'

'I'm sure you won't have any more trouble.' He went to the French doors and checked the screen, then turned slowly and looked at her. 'Well, what do you think?'

'I think someone deliberately tried to frighten me —or worse.'

'Well then, you just let me attend to it.' His expression was hard and to Rosanne's way of thinking, quite frightening. For a devastating moment she realised she didn't know him at all.

'You don't believe Francine did it?' Her green eyes were huge and brilliant. 'No woman in her right mind would pick up a snake, especially a tiger snake.'

'No, Francine didn't do it.' Ross compressed his mouth. 'Surely you don't really want a cup of tea?'

'Yes, I *do*!' Rosanne still had shuddery sensations along her spine.

'Then come along.' He shook his head faintly. 'And before you do, put some clothes on, for God's sake. Sheer nighties are a riot, but they let out the wild beast in a man.'

Incredibly Francine was gone in the morning and Marta explained that Ross had flown her back to Malawarra. Mrs Curtis came in from the kitchen, put fresh coffee down and Marta paused, then waited until the housekeeper had gone out of the breakfast room again.

'She's been crying.' Rosanne made the comment in spite of herself; for the housekeeper's normally stern, controlled face was blurred with a spent agony of tears.

'Poor thing!' Marta dropped her eyes. 'I'm afraid she's all wound up about her dreadful son. Ross ran him off the property.'

'Whatever for?' Rosanne went cold with guilt. It was *her* fault.

'What do we care?' Sharyn answered quietly for her mother. 'He's no good. In fact he'd do anything to make a dollar.'

'He told me he was desperate!' Rosanne pushed her plate away. She had completely lost her appetite.

'I expect his mother gave him all she had. Dale has caused her a lot of worry, but he won't be coming here again. Mrs Curtis knows this and she understands. We don't want to lose her. She's extremely efficient and she values her job.'

'So we're minus Francine and Dale?'

'You bet!' Sharyn suddenly jumped to her feet. 'And don't think for a moment *I'm* going to grieve. When you're finished, girls, we'll start on all those invitations.'

Rosanne had to give in. No one would listen to her, anyway, and now that she saw how much pleasure Marta and Sharyn were deriving from their plans, she no longer considered herself at all. Perhaps, afterwards, Ross would let her go. She would have to speak to him about it. She had kept to her part of the bargain. Marta was feeling and looking so much better and free from the rigid misery that had pervaded her days, able to be a mother to her daughter.

A week went by and Rosanne finally gathered the courage to speak to Ross. It was a battle to speak to him in any case. She had ridden down to the yards constantly during the week, but there was always some incident or some hand trying to speak to him and she had always ridden away without saying a word. Running a big station seemed to be a twenty-four-hour business, and then at night there were the books.

The only thing she could do was beard the lion in his den. She even had an extra glass of wine at dinner to do it. Though she loved this life, the excitement and freedom, she was her own person and her self-respect was important to her. Maybe Ross didn't think she had any, but she did.

Outside his study she stood for a moment rehearsing what she was going to say. If the truth was known, she was really quite frightened of him, which was ridiculous. All she had to do was speak with composure and dignity. She had come to High Valley to give comfort to Robin's mother, and she had accomplished that. There had been no suggestion that she should stay, and no dancer could afford to be away from their own world for any length of time.

She knocked on the door and when he answered, she started. Damn Ross! Much as she loved him he made her incredibly nervous.

When she entered the room, he stood up and came around the massive, richly carved desk. 'Come into my parlour, said the spider to the fly.'

'May I speak to you, please, Ross?' she asked formally.

'That's all you *can* do!' His voice was suddenly sensuous and mocking.

'May I sit down?'

'Sure, over there, where I can look at you.'

Rosanne flushed a little at the expression in his eyes, then moved back to sit in the big leather chair. It was comfortable, but too big perhaps. She felt lost.

'I like your dress.' He wasn't coming to her rescue.

'I think you've given me too much.' She stared moodily at her champagne silk skirt. It was a very pretty dress, already a favourite, and she could never have afforded it by herself.

'Don't look so censorious. You're not a kept woman because you've been forced into accepting a few dresses. They're enormously alluring.'

She had to ignore the deliberate mockery in his tone. 'Ross, I want to know when you're going to let me go.'

'Go where, baby?' His silver eyes glinted.

'Back to my own world!' She actually jumped up to confront him. 'I've done everything you asked me to do.'

'Yes, you have,' he answered coolly, 'so I find myself wondering why I'm going to say no.'

'*No?*' She could feel herself shaking. 'I don't understand!'

'I've got to be sure. Don't you see that?'

'I know Marta will miss me,' she protested, 'but she has you and Sharyn.'

'Except she wants you to stay a little longer.'

'I *can't*, Ross.' Desperation made her say it a little wildly.

'Why not?' He put out his hands and encircled her narrow waist.

'I've been away from the company too long.'

'Away from André?' His face changed, hardened, and he looked damned good-looking and impossibly arrogant.

'Do I have to remind you André meant nothing to me!' When she needed to have her mind clear it was fogging with desire.

'Ah well, he considers you, his — *friend*.' The warmth of his hands was penetrating the silk material, but still he held her pinned.

'I'll leave all the same,' she huskily. 'I can't just drift.'

'I thought you were enjoying it.' He moved her closer so she was right up against him as he leant back on the desk.

'I know how you feel about me,' she said tormentedly. 'You're a sadist!'

'A *what*?' He propelled her forward and kissed her open mouth.

'*Please*, Ross!' She was terrified of her mounting ardour. The flame he lit that made pride and common sense no more. She could see herself falling into his arms, her hair floating around both of them. Why didn't he let her go when he could feel she was so frightened?

His hand was moving up caressingly along her back, arching her against him while his kiss slowed from a faint savagery to a deep, lingering hunger. Rosanne couldn't fight him. How could she, when she wanted this herself.

'What am I going to do about you, Rosie?' he muttered against the creamy column of her throat.

He sounded almost angry and it moved her to try and pull away. She didn't have to be a willing victim, yet some part of him wanted her and he couldn't pretend otherwise.

'I can't bear what you're trying to do to me,' she whispered. 'It's cruel.'

'I know how it is.' He put his hand, then his mouth to her breast.

She couldn't help it, she moaned. Even through the silk the excitement was fierce, blotting out caution.

'Just how long do you think *this* is going to satisfy me?' he asked harshly.

'You can't....' she managed that much of a denial before his mouth cut her of ruthlessly and he lifted her and moved backwards towards the magnificent leather-upholstered chesterfield.

It was the same for both of them; the loss of control. All the critical messages her brain had been sending to her body were forgotten. Ross's heart was pounding into her own, rendering her incapable of doing anything except pressing her trembling, yearning body closer to his.

Then Ross surprised her by jerking her head back, his muscles coiled, his silver eyes as wary as any big cat in a jungle. 'Tell me about Robin.' His voice was hard, and compulsively menacing.

She couldn't even answer and he pulled painfully on her hair. 'I want to know, little one. No lies.'

Rosanne blinked rapidly, her green, black-fringed eyes clearly bewildered. 'I really cared for Robin. Not like *this*. . . .'

'Did you tell him you loved him?' he interrupted impatiently.

'I thought I did.' She was half stretched across him and he was holding her face.

'Except you didn't sleep with him?'

'No, I didn't.' She was suddenly angry herself. 'There are some men who are prepared to wait!'

'Only it wasn't typical of Robin.'

'Well then, I never gave him a chance!' She was crazy to think he would ever believe her about anything.

'Dammit, you little witch, you need proof!' He stood up so suddenly she tumbled in front of him, half lying on the Persian rug as he walked away from her to the ceiling-high panelled shelves that held books. He had to reach up and a leather-bound book fell, striking him on the shoulder, but he took no notice. It was another book he wanted and he pulled it out roughly and kept hold of it.

'What's that?' Rosanne stood up, searching his face.

'The letter I got from Robin a few days before his death.'

'*Show me.*' She felt so dizzy she thought she would faint. 'I have a right to know.'

'Aren't you afraid?' His silver eyes almost slashed at her.

'No. I have no reason to be!' She put out her hand, though every nerve in her body was jumping.

'I've tried to erase it from my mind,' he said tautly.

'*Please*, give it to me,' she begged with young dignity.

'I think you'd better take it to your room. Afterwards, you'll want to destroy it.'

'Why didn't you?' The pain showed in her eyes.

'Because nothing went as I planned,' he said raspingly. 'My God, *nothing.*'

He let her go without another word and she carried the book with the letter in it up to her room. Had Robin gone insane? What could he possible write of her that could cause his stepbrother to hate and despise her? She felt her face contort as she heard Dale Curtis's voice telling her Robin had learnt hate long ago. Could he have been revenging himself on his brother, through her? But how and why?

The letter was the answer. She was safely in her room now and she turned on the lights. Now as always, she looked away to see the screen door to the balcony was shut, then, as she walked to the bed, she caught side of her face in the dressing table mirror. She looked remarkable, incandescent. And she was amazed that it could be so.

The leather-bound book was a copy of Dostoevsky's *Crime and Punishment*, and she wondered bitterly if Ross had selected it deliberately. The letter was inside in Robin's rambling hand, and Rosanne unfolded the pages and began to read.

By the time she came to the end of the first page, distress had turned her paper-white. This wasn't Robin! He had to be ill. She knew Robin. He couldn't write these terrible lies.

There was another page; a third, a fourth and a fifth. She could hear the watch on her wrist ticking very loudly. Her body was numb; she had no feeling in it at all. The worse the things she read, the colder she became. It couldn't touch her, all this treachery.

'I'm quite calm,' she said aloud. 'I'll forget Robin. Forget the man I love. Forget I ever came to High Valley.' What Robin had written she couldn't show to another living soul, yet believing it, Ross had brought her into his home. She remembered now the way Robin had laughed that night. He had been strung up, gay, forgiving her her imaginary affair with André. She remembered too, he had driven so fast it had made her frightened, until laughingly he had stopped.

'Nearly killed you then, didn't I, darling?'

She remembered his very words.

Had he tried to kill her? None of it mattered now to her at all; he had destroyed her anyway. Very quickly she tore the letter to pieces in short, jerky movements. He had created a very clever picture of her, all innocence—and *underneath*. How could he have ever said he loved her? How could she ever prove all he had said was lies, unless she gave herself in an experiment without love. It was unthinkable, and now she began to feel sick at the pit of her stomach. No matter how much it hurt Marta, she had to get away.

She slept badly and in the morning she knew she had to confront Ross again. Getting off High Valley would be impossible without his aid. The station was so isolated, though freight planes flew in. She would have to explain her departure rather than affront Marta's hospitality. Completely unable to send a telegram to herself, she could say dancing was the love of her life and she was missing it badly. Marta would be upset and disappointed, but no matter. Her life on High Valley was over.

Sharyn commented on her wan face at breakfast and Rosanne explained it away as a slight headache.

She was going out in any case and the breeze would blow it away.

'We've heard from Julie,' Marta told her delightedly. 'She's flying in at the weekend.'

An hour later Rosanne slipped out quietly and though she wanted to be on her own, Curly stubbornly refused to let her out of his sight.

'The boss'll kill me,' he said, and shook his head.

'Very well, come along,' shrugged Rosanne.

' 'Scuse me, Miss Rosanne, you look pale.'

'It's all right, Curly, I'm fit enough.'

'Where are we goin'?' Curly asked. 'Yah don't mind tellin' me, I suppose?'

Rosanne flushed, glanced back at him and smiled. 'I want to see Mr McAdam.'

'Oh.' Curly frowned doubtfully. 'He's kinda busy today.'

'I'm going to speak to him all the same.'

'Right, miss!' Curly gave a cackle of laughter. 'I think you've got somethin' on your mind.'

Rosanne nodded in an absent way and turned Lady around. Ross would realise now she had to go. Curly, too, swung his horse about, settled his ancient slouch hat further down over his eyes and they rode out. It was very hot and banks of cloud were rolling in from the Gulf.

They tried the first camp, then the second, and one of the old black stockmen with snow-white hair and a white beard told them the Boss was moving cattle in from the plain.

'Don't reckon we should go any further!' Curly shifted back in the saddle and stared up at the sky. 'We could have a storm.'

'Perhaps he's on the other side of the lagoon.' Rosanne wiped the perspiration from her temples with her bandana.

'Are yah sure this is important, miss?' Curly asked her kindly.

'I'm certain we'll find him.' Her small face looked pale and exhausted.

'All right, then, we'll make for the next camp, but that's all. Yah can't expect the Boss to understand if I slip up the third time.'

Rosanne shook her head. 'It's never been your fault.'

Above the screeching of the cockatoos they heard the distant bellowing of cattle and Rosanne's face brightened. 'Come on, Curly, let's go!'

Curly said nothing. He just rose up on his stirrups and scanned the countryside. 'Over there,' he pointed a skinny hand. 'We'll probably find him over there.'

They were less than a hundred yards from the camp when a clap of thunder tore the darkening sky.

'Struth, that's done it!' she heard Curly gasp.

A half a dozen stockmen were staring their way, but when they heard the thunder they moved quickly to their horses. The birds had stopped screeching now and there was an unearthly stillness after that first drum roll.

A rider whipped into camp, swung out of the saddle and came up to Rosanne, tightly holding Lady's reins. 'You bloody fool, Curly, why did you bring her here?'

'Don't blame me, Boss,' he yelled. On the other side of the camp the mob were bellowing their fear of the thunder.

'I *had* to see you, Ross.' Rosanne felt confounded by his anger, the tension in the faces of the men.

'Get with the men, Curly,' Ross called curtly. 'We don't want a stampede on our hands.'

'Right!' Curly waited for no more, but rode across to join the stockboys.

'Get down off there,' Ross told her savagely, and as she hesitated, every nerve tight, he swore violently and lifted her bodily out of the saddle. 'Why you'd pick today to come out after me I'd never know!'

'So what's wrong with a thunderstorm?'

'I haven't got time to tell you.' He swung around and shouted orders to the men, all the while propelling Rosanne along so she was half off the ground. 'Get up that tree,' he said quickly. 'Come on, I'll throw you up.'

'What's happening?' The tension seemed to be increasing around them and the bellow of the frightened beasts had her shouting over the inferno of sound.

'Damn it, get up!' Ross got her around the waist, such strength in his wrists and arms she was almost flung on to the safety of a heavy branch. 'Get higher!'

There was such fury and urgency in his shout that she didn't dare disobey. Holding on to the branches above her, she climbed until she could look down on the camp.

Ross was already in the saddle, wheeling his splendid black mare around, then it bounded forward as a stricken beast made a wild dash into the camp. Instantly he headed it off and rounded it back, and just at that moment the rumbling thunder surged into one almighty clap that shocked Rosanne so much she covered her ears.

All the men were wheeling their horses now, stockwhips in hand as the Boss snapped commands, then as the heavens opened, three hundred and more terrified, milling cattle were suddenly galvanised into action.

The leaders moved off in uncontrollable fear and

immediately the mob surged behind them in a bovine panic, sweeping right through the campsite in a bellowing frenzy, scattering and pounding into dust everything in sight.

Rosanne had the terrible conviction all of them would never live through it; men and horses pressing into the mob, moving at the precise minute to avoid the murderous slash of horns. The whole sight was full of a terrible peril. She would never forget it—the raw power, the rain and the wind, the bellowing, the crack and lash of the stockwhips, the frantic yells of the men.

Heavy grey and red-brown bodies pounded beneath her tree and she could feel the ground shaking so violently she was terrified the tree would be uprooted. She was drenched now, covered in the sweat of fear and the rain, braced every minute to be flung out on to the ground.

She could hear the men's curses and her staring eyes witnessed their superb horsemanship. She had only caught sight of Ross once, galloping up beside the lead bullock. He was well ahead now and she prayed desperately he would be safe. To be caught by those horns! To be slashed to ribbons, then trampled. Death seemed so close and a man and his horse could easily be borne down under the shocking momentum of the stampede. One second's miscalculation! Rosanne was almost paralysed with fear—not for herself, her danger was now past, but for Ross and the men.

She didn't know how long it took for the tumult and shouting to die away. She clung to her branch, praying, tortured by the thought that any one of them could have met a violent death. As suddenly as the heavens had opened up, the rain had turned off and the churned-up earth was steaming with heat.

The sun was beating down again and she eased herself gradually down the tree, filled with a terrible unease. If anything had happened to Ross!

She had to jump to the ground and she saw now that she was up in mud to her ankles. Her eyes flicked round the camp, smashed timber, broken branches swinging crazily. In such a short space of time, a deluge and a stampede. Curly had told her hair-raising stories she had discounted much of, but never again. Behind the nonchalance of the lone horseman was a life full of danger.

She thought for a few moments what she should do, then as she stood quakingly, Ross rode back into the ravaged camp.

Thank God you're safe! Her thoughts were in her green eyes, but she couldn't get a word out of her throat.

'Your first stampede,' he told her. 'It's all over.'

'And no one was hurt?' she croaked.

'Robbie's hurt his leg.'

Rosanne seemed dazed and he put out his hand urgingly. 'Come on up with me, I'll take you back to the house.'

She nodded dumbly, accepting his help to climb into the saddle in front of him. 'And Lady?' she asked.

'She knows how to dodge trouble. Unfortunately I can't say the same for you.' Ross hauled her back against him.

'I *had* to talk to you.'

'You picked a bloody funny time,' he observed.

'Okay, so I did. I'm sorry.'

'I believe you. You've got a very expressive face.'

Reduced, both physically and mentally, Rosanne had to rest against him and his arm tightened around her waist.

'Where do we go from here, little one?'

'Each to our own world,' she said painfully, aware that the best part of her would always remain with him.

'Take off that silly hat!' He brought his hand up and flung her sodden hat away. 'I doubt very much if you know your own destiny.'

Rosanne didn't make any reply and he urged the mare into a gallop. The beautiful animal took off, as fleet as the breeze, such magic in motion that Rosanne found herself responding to the experience irresistibly.

'Please, would you let me try her?' she shouted into the wind.

'Never, my infant.' Set at a fallen log ahead, the mare sailed over it. 'God forbid you should break your pretty neck.'

She turned her head and looked back and up at him, noting the twist to his mouth. 'Isn't that one way to make me pay?'

'Oh, yes,' his eyes were hooded so she was uncertain of their expression, 'but I've thought of another.'

The mare's powerful long legs were eating up the savannah and as they came within a few hundred yards of the main compound, they saw Nada's slight figure on an unsaddled workhorse.

'Missa Ross!' The wind lifted her pealing tones, carrying their overtones of urgency.

'God, what's wrong now?' Ross dug in his heels and the mare jumped forward with a great leap.

'Missa Ross!' They were on Nada now and they could see the stark apprehension in her face. 'Come quickly, it's Missus McAdam!'

CHAPTER EIGHT

ROSANNE arrived at the rehearsal hall a full half hour before most of the others. Barakat was there, the balletmaster, and he started her in almost immediately on barre work. It was Friday morning and the gala opening of *Giselle* was that night. In a way, that was all she had, her work.

'Perfection, darling!' Barakat kissed his hand to her, then immediately turned around and screeched at one of the kids from the corps de ballet. 'Imbecile!' he cried with sadistic delight.

Rosanne scarcely heard him, her breakable body sheened with sweat. She had never worked harder in her life; never weighed in so light.

'Darling, darling,' Barakat called to her, 'save something for the performance!'

She slowed her tempo and Damien at the rehearsal piano stopped his frenzied pounding and fed her mood music. She looked across the rehearsal room at him and smiled, then she soared into a magical leap. It looked so perfect, so easy, yet it had taken her years to lift like a leaf in the wind. Tonight, if she could keep body and soul together, she would dance Giselle. She would have André to help her. He would be her Albrecht and they danced beautifully together, the choreography so familiar to them they could almost forget about it and allow their acting to become real.

The rehearsal went on. André joined her and they went through the pas de deux of the first act, André's true feelings towards her so patent, it lent an almost unbearable poignancy to their first expression of youthful, doomed love. Rosanne, for her part, was acting, but acting with the passionate intensity that made her a perfect partner. She knew all about doomed love. Every day for long months now she had had a silvery sword at her breast. So tonight, when she picked up the sword of her lover to fall on it, a lot of her anguish would be real.

Afterwards she and André stood quietly, well wrapped up to prevent chilled muscles and watched the Wilis rehearsing. Sondra, who played the Queen of the Wilis, flitted smoothly across the floor, but it still didn't please Barakat, who swore at her and told her she moved as effortlessly as a 'fat cow'. Sondra took it well, waved a hand at him and tried it again. Even out of costume, it look ghostly.

The new boy, Brett Hansen, was dancing the part of Hilarion, and though it wasn't a big role, he was bringing a degree of excellence to it that had André narrowing his black eyes.

'He dances well.'

'Not so well as you.' It was a routine compliment, but André seemed to need it. Soon Rosanne would go on again, the great solo of the second act, changed from an innocent and love-struck young girl to a terrifyingly cold and brilliant Wili, the ghost of a girl who had been betrayed.

But he didn't betray me! Her private thoughts matched the tragedy. Desire wasn't love, and Ross had never ever mentioned such a word. It had ended just as it had started and for months now she had been filled with such heartache it showed visibly, opening up such a range of emotions; her every bal-

letic gesture born of joy or love or sorrow left no one in
the Company unmoved. In time, the Director had told
her, she would make a great dancer, but now such a
pinnacle no longer seemed a glittering prize. Falling in
love with Ross had been a disaster and she lived with it
day in and day out. Now, to dance, to dance beautifully, wasn't enough.

'Darling, you're not crying?' André tilted her pale
little face.

'Of course not.' She smiled at him with her great
green eyes. 'I expect it's mascara.'

'Ah, yes, mascara.' André touched her quivering
shoulder. 'I would be willing to kill him, this man who
has made you suffer.'

'I'd adore it if you two would pay attention!' Barakat
called out to them indignantly, and André responded
a little crudely under his breath.

'I'd better be off, then, darling!' He glanced sideways at Rosanne and smiled at her. 'After the performance I'm going to treat you to the most wonderful
supper.'

'Damn it, André,' Barakat was losing his cool,
'would you pull yourself away from Giselle and come
here. If you don't *mind*, that is.'

'Coming, my love!' André gave his wicked urchin
smile. He often answered Barakat like this and now as
always the balletmaster shook his fists. It was extremely hard to decide what to do about André.

'Damn silly, stupid girl!' Bakarat retaliated by
picking on a little Wili who had been working well
all morning. 'Do we have a performance tonight or
not?'

The response of that first night National Ballet
Theatre audience was all any of them could have
wanted, from the Director down to the humblest

member of the corps de ballet. It was a very special night with an almost full house, and as the leading critic, Gregory Nixon, later put it, the whole company had never danced better. The enchanting Rosanne Grey had given an infinitely satisfying performance in a role that seemed made for her, and although there were words of high praise for André, Brett Hansen's small role was called a 'show-piece'.

To Rosanne and André, standing alone on the stage after their fifth curtain call, the applause came in great waves. Members of the audience were on their feet cheering, and as Rosanne looked out over the gala crowd, her great eyes brilliant and enhanced by her stage make-up, her rapidly beating heart almost stopped in shock.

There was a man out there, a tall man with a thick shock of black hair and startling light blue eyes. She gave an involuntary gasp and as she continued to stare in his direction he lifted his right hand in salute.

'Bravo!' The audience were shouting their praise now, not a one of them attempting to leave. André lifted her hand to kiss it and as was her custom she selected a single, perfect rose from her beautiful sheaf of roses and handed it to him with exquisite grace.

'They adore you, darling,' André said ardently. 'Us!'

If she didn't get off the stage she would faint. The curtain fell again, went up as the bravos continued, then as Rosanne and André retreated, still smiling, it came down for the last time.

The Director walked up suddenly and kissed Rosanne on both cheeks, and it was only the beginning of the adulation. There were admirers galore. Feverishly her eyes ranged over the laughing, congratulatory crowd of dancers and balletgoers that ringed her round, but there was no sign of the tall dark man she had stared at with so much fascination. With the footlights in her eyes she had fantasised that man had been Ross. Ross—oh God! She couldn't breathe for the physical pain. Tonight she had pushed herself to the limit and instead of being filled with elation she wanted to leap right off the edge of the world. She must know by now that she would never see Ross again.

Finally she was alone in her dressing room with her own face looking back at her, or her own face made compulsively haunting in her overstated make-up. Her eyes were like jewels, consuming her face, and whatever happened, she decided, she would not cry. She had done all her crying after Marta had died. Dear, kind Marta whose heart hadn't proved strong enough. Rosanne had felt her death deeply, though Sharyn and Julie had both tried to comfort her by saying she, Rosanne, had brought peace and happiness back into their mother's life. It had happened so suddenly, with Marta aglow with her plans, then while she was tending the orchids she loved she had collapsed.

Those had been black days. Impossible days. The end of a dream.

Wincing a little, she took off her pink satin shoes, next, her beautiful, traditional full-skirted white dress. There was a party afterwards to go to. A *party*! She didn't have the heart. Very neat and methodical, she put her costume away. Costumes were expensive and they required careful handling.

Next, with her green silk robe on, she sat down at the dressing table and prepared to turn herself back into Rosanne Grey. The role of Giselle had been affecting her, a triumph for the Company, but not the healthiest role for an unhappy young girl.

The cold cream removed the make-up, but she avoided her eyes for the time being. Unless she could wash her face directly afterwards the cold cream got into her eyes and made them sore. They looked very extravagant in her white face, but she didn't care. She would make her apologies to the rest of them and go back to her apartment. André would be deeply disappointed. He might insist that she come, but she would have to plead a bad headache. If she was going to be famous, there would be plenty of parties.

There was a knock at the door, and thinking it was André, she steeled herself to turn him down. André had been a good friend to her, more than half way in love with her, largely perhaps because she remained elusive, but she could never, for whatever reason, embark on an affair. She had found her one, perfect love and he hadn't wanted her.

As she called a husky, '*Entrez!*' the door opened in and a man entered. A tall man as sleek and handsome as a big, jungle cat.

'*Ross!*' He loomed behind her in the mirror and she could only sit there staring back at his reflection.

'I wish I could tell you how much pleasure you gave me.'

The sound of his voice was like a scream of pain along her nerves.

'It *was* you, then?' She sounded breathless.

'Why don't you turn around and find out?'

She shook her head, her heart pounding heavily. 'Why don't you just leave me alone? It wasn't kind of you, Ross, to come here.' Belatedly she stood up and pulled the sash of her robe tighter around her tiny waist. 'I suppose you're here on business for a few days?'

'I'm damned if I really know!' His silver eyes were watching her and she thought fleetingly that he looked strangely at home in elegant evening clothes.

'How's Sharyn, Julie?' Was that her voice sounding so brittle?

'They're fine, and they send their love.'

She wanted to laugh at that, wondering why she felt slightly hysterical. 'I suppose they asked you to call on me?'

'No,' he said a little shortly, and extended an arm to stop her aimless pacing. 'You were wonderful tonight, a revelation. I know very little of ballet, but it seems to me you have all it takes to make a great dancer.'

'Of course—that's what I've always wanted to be!' Unbelievably she was able to look quite coolly into his eyes. If she was careful now, she could play a most brilliant part.

'Are you happy?' Ross suddenly brought his hand up to cup her chin.

'Damn you, Ross, who's happy!' She jerked away, trying desperately not to react to his touch.

'My sisters are. They've been worried about you since you haven't returned their letters.'

'I've been busy.' She flushed painfully.

'I'm sure you have.' There was a brilliant, cold sparkle in his eyes. 'I'd be terrified to ask what weight you are now.'

'Oh, I'm healthy, be sure of that.' She moved further away from him, but it was too small a room.

'I think tonight, you're the most beautiful thing I've ever seen.'

'Not some vista on High Valley?' She whirled around to challenge him.

'I've hurt you, haven't I?' he said quietly.

'Ah well. . . .' Despite herself the bitterness crept into her voice. 'We were never exactly friends.'

'What did we have for each other anyway?' She

saw the tightened muscles along his jaw.

'So I assume it was curiosity that brought you along tonight?'

'It proved something anyway,' he laughed harshly. 'You'll probably end up being famous.'

There was a tap on the door and as they both twisted around, André put his head around, wearing a brilliant smile.

'Ah, you have a visitor!' The smile cleared in an instant, and the mobile face looked as dazed as Rosanne felt.

'How are you, LeStrange?' Ross put out his hand more than a full head over André, and André took it, obviously incapable of resisting the overture.

'Fine, thank you.' André's dark eyes swept from one to the other. 'I didn't think you cared for ballet.'

'Nevertheless I stood up and shouted bravo tonight.'

'How kind of you to say so.' André's mood began to improve. It was impossible to mistake genuine admiration. 'You're staying in town?'

'For at least another day.' Ross leaned back against a wardrobe looking very smooth and relaxed. 'I've been trying to persuade Rosanne to allow me to take her out to supper.'

'But what a pity! She's coming to the party.'

'Oh damn. . . .' Ross looked deeply disappointed.

'But it's a big party and of course you can come.' André spread his expressive hands. 'I expect it will be a very long time before you see Rosanne again.'

Rosanne moved fretfully, her control slipping. 'I'm sorry, really, both of you, but I have a terrible head.'

'Why didn't you tell me?' André's dark eyes flashed with concern.

'I hate to disappoint you, I really do, but it could be a migraine.'

'Then I must take you home!' André responded gallantly as always.

'I wish you'd allow me,' Ross said persuasively, 'I'm pressed for time and there's so much Rosanne and I have to catch up on. My stepsister is getting engaged at the end of the month and of course we want Rosanne to fly up to us.'

'Oh,' said André with reserve, 'in *that* case——'

'Congratulations again for a wonderful performance.'

'It wasn't at all bad,' André agreed warmly. 'Of course I had my little Rose. It makes a performance to have the perfect partner.' He walked across and kissed the top of Rosanne's shining head. 'Poor little lamb! You've been having too many of these headaches lately.'

'She's certainly got thinner, and she's lost all her colour,' Ross observed dispassionately.

'This is what comes of driving oneself too hard.' André spoke slowly and thoughtfully. 'Sure I can't get you something?'

'No, it's all right.' Rosanne looked up at him and smiled this time. 'Could you make my apologies for me?'

'Everyone will be so disappointed.'

'There'll be other nights!' Ross pointed out suavely. 'Surely the best thing I could do now is get her home.'

'Perhaps you're right!' André murmured in an uncertain tone, glancing back and forth from one closed face to the other. He knew perfectly well Ross McAdam was directly responsible for his partner's unhappiness, yet McAdam too looked as if he had been driving himself hard.

After André had gone, Rosanne said nothing. She stood with a bent head reminding herself forcibly

if she valued what little peace of mind she had she
would have to reject Ross's offer to drive her home.

'Aren't you going to get dressed?' he asked.

'I don't know that I'm in any great hurry.' He was so
vivid, so sophisticated and self-assured, it was painful
to watch him.

'Well, *I* am!' he said with a quick return to his old
forcefulness. 'Let's get away from this place, go somewhere and talk. Back to your apartment.'

'Honestly, I can't think what we have to talk about.'
She was trying to insult him so she could endure her
own pain.

'Oh, you can tell me what you've been doing these
last miserable months.'

'Oh, for heaven's sake!' Her green eyes blazed
and she picked up her dress and went behind the
screen. 'One never knows what a man like you is up
to.'

Somehow Ross had managed to park his late
model hire car almost directly opposite the theatre
and he pulled out into the heavy traffic with effortless skill.

'Where to?' he asked.

Rosanne named the close into town suburb automatically, not in the least surprised when he told her
he knew how to find it. Ross could find anything, any
time. He had found her.

He parked in her private bay and she found herself
walking to her front door in a daze, his hard hand at
her elbow.

'What the devil are you doing living here?' In the
brightly lit exterior she could see the frown lines between his winged brows.

'I can't help it if it doesn't come up to your standard.
It's actually quite a pleasant place to live for a struggling dancer.'

'God!' He cut her short, shaking his head. 'Give me that key. That's the second time you've tried to insert it.'

It was true. She was trembling too much with the shock of their encounter.

Inside the modest apartment was something different again. Rosanne had rented it unfurnished and transformed it into a fascinating retreat. It was a highly individual form of decorating, unaffectedly feminine, and it said style and personality for a limited budget.

Ross walked about without saying anything, prowling it seemed like a panther in a cage.

'Can I get you anything? A drink?' asked Rosanne.

'More to the point, what can I get you?' He picked up a piece of sculpture and put it down.

'I'm just tired, period.' She put a hand to her cheek, still shiny with cream. 'If you'll excuse me a moment, I'll get all this cream off my face. There's some Scotch in the cabinet over there and some ice cubes in the fridge if you want them.'

She turned away without another word and disappeared into the bedroom. Why was he here? Her thoughts were in an uproar. She had to be absolutely crazy to let Ross inside her door. She was still standing beside her bed in a kind of stupor that broke under a torrent of self-disgust.

So what did he think she would do? Fall into his arms?

Violently she pinned her hair on top of her head and stripped her slender body naked. It would be just as easy to have a quick shower as wash her face.

The force of the jet of water took her mind off her fury. She soaped herself quickly and for a final rinse turned off the hot water. It brought her right to her senses. She would show Ross she wasn't the romantic

little fool he thought she was. Most girls were entitled to an enormous crush, and she had been a late
bloomer.

When she came out of the shower she was still mut-
tering under her breath, nevertheless the tap on her
door shocked her.

'What the hell are you doing in there?'
Ross's voice was loaded with a barely contained im-
patience.

'Doing... *doing*....' she muttered in a rage. There
was nothing new in hearing him speaking to her so
harshly. Besides which, *let him wait*!

The door flew open and he was standing on the
threshold, a flicker of anxiety on his dark face.

'Do you *mind*?' The hardest part was to cover herself, but mercifully it was a very large towel.

'You didn't say anything about taking a shower!'

'Very well. I had a shower, now I'm trying to get
dressed.' A paroxysm of hysterical laughter gurgled up
from her throat.

'All right, I'll go.' His silver eyes lanced over her,
the careless topknot, long gilt stands hanging down,
outraged eyes, silky skin, pink, fluffy towel. 'Hurry
up.'

The door shut again and just in case he had a mind
to come back again, Rosanne raced to the wardrobe
and pulled out a robe that zipped right up to the neck.
A gold tasselled cord went around her waist and she
had gold bedroom slippers some place. She found
them under the bed and stepped into them quickly.
How dared Ross walk in on her? How dared he let his
glance dwell on her like that? She walked to the dressing table, picked up her brush and ran it through her
hair in a tingling rush. All kinds of emotions were
sweeping her, frightful delusions that he still wanted
her.

When she walked back into the living room, he was looking at an abstract painting she had hung on the wall. He had removed his jacket and when he turned around she saw he had further made himself comfortable by taking off his black silk bow tie and unbuttoning his white, ruffled evening shirt.

He looked very handsome, slightly rakish, and she felt unable to cope with anything, let alone him.

'How do you feel now?' he asked solicitously.

'Much better.'

'No head?' One black eyebrow shot up.

'I never had one in the first place,' she said irritably. 'I just wanted to come home.'

'You're an unlikely prima ballerina. I thought they thrived on adulation?'

'I think there's something wrong with me,' she answered wryly, 'Why are you here, Ross?'

'So crisp and businesslike? Come here.'

'No. Keep away.' Her voice had gone husky.

'I have, actually. For a long time.' He picked up his crystal tumbler, drained it and put it down on the Italian coffee table. 'I thought of you every day.'

'Okay, so I cried every night.' She shrugged her shoulder with some of his own cynicism.

'What hysterically or just plain getting over?'

'I'd really rather not discuss it.'

'Then come over here and sit down.'

She didn't move but stood there like a figurine. 'Are you going back to High Valley tomorrow?' she asked.

'I don't know. I think I'll come and see you again.'

'I'm not dancing tomorrow night.'

'Then I'll drop around for dinner.' His teasing voice carried undercurrents that rocked her and she went over to the stereo, turned it on and let the music play softly.

'I'm afraid I'm not much of a cook.' Actually she was a good one.

'Then we'll go out. That is if you haven't stopped eating altogether?' His silver eyes glinted over her.

'So I've lost weight,' she shrugged.

'Come over here and we'll talk about it?'

'So tell me what's been happening to you?' she ignored his invitation and sank down on to the velvet-upholstered sofa, tucking her feet under her. 'How's Francine?'

'Somewhat better.' His eyes dwelt on the soft curves of her mouth. 'There's a new romantic possibility in her life.'

'Then we can only hope he's not as dilatory as you.'

'Dilatory, for God's sake!' A faint sexual hostility stirred in his face. 'My story's the classic one—love at first sight.'

'And I suppose you're still damning her to hell,' she returned vehemently.

'It's a normal reaction on the part of the male.'

He stood up and she couldn't control her nervous start. 'Am I going to hear this paragon's name?' she asked.

'You will.' His face took on a guarded look. 'The trouble is I don't know if I've got the right to uproot her.'

'You mean she doesn't love you?' she asked jerkily, more desperately unhappy than she had ever been in her life.

'Let's find out.'

She had scarcely a minute to register warning signals before he scooped her up, then lowered himself back on to the sofa again, enclosing her in his arms.

'Don't, Ross!' she protested. 'This is crazy!'

'I know, and it rankles.' His fingers traced the contours of her face and brushed her quivering lips. 'God, I'll go mad if you don't kiss me.'

'Kiss you when you're going to marry another woman?' Her voice rose in a mad rage.

'I'd rather carry you off instead.' He speared his fingers through her hair and pulled her head back. 'I swear I'll live like a monk if I can't have you.'

Her shock and lack of comprehension was such that she began to struggle wildly, and he closed his steel arms around her and found her mouth.

'*Rosanne!*'

She couldn't match his passion, she was trembling so much. 'Yes, it's *me*!' She jerked her mouth away. 'Haven't you damaged me enough?'

'Be quiet.' He said it sternly. 'There's no other woman but you. No one since my eyes fell on you.'

She didn't answer; she couldn't, for her heart had turned over in her breast.

'It's been too long, Rosanne,' Ross murmured, and bent his head.

This time she knew better than to try to crush her desire, and her body that had been rigid yielded like warm silk in his arms. Ross loved her. She couldn't really understand it, but he gave her no possible reason to believe otherwise. Her trembling had extended to him and while he still held her with his mouth his hand found the zip on her robe and moved it until it fell to her waist.

She was naked beneath the satin and now he knew it too, his strong hands cupping her breasts.

'I love you.'

Rosanne closed her eyes, letting him hold her so his mouth could move back and forth across her skin. It was a frantic feeling having him hold her in this way, yet wonderful tears filled her eyes. For long

months now there had been nothing for her but heartache, now she was afraid she couldn't contain her
deep hunger.

'Tell me you love me, Rosanne?' He kissed the
soft hollow at the base of her throat.

'I thought I'd told you from the very beginning.'

'*Say* it.' He hurt her just a little.

'I love you.' She drew herself up to say it against
his mouth.

'Enough to give up your career?' His hands came
up to hold her face in his hands.

'You w—want me to?' Her green eyes were so soft
and shimmering with love.

He shook his head. 'Half of me feels I haven't got
the right.'

'And the other half?' She pressed little butterfly
kisses from his cheekbone down to the corner of his
mouth.

'The other half couldn't bear to have you out of
my sight.'

'Do you trust me?' she whispered.

His hand left her face and sought her breast. 'I
do.'

'You didn't once.' She gave a little convulsive
shudder, her body stirring unbearably yet wanting to
question him.

'I didn't want to.' He pulled her back so she was
lying against him. 'I found myself hating the way I
felt about you. To have a woman move in right under
my heart was like surrendering up part of myself, and
I've been a very independent man.'

'And now?' His caresses were taking her past control.

'And now I don't think I could bear to wake up
in the morning without finding you beside me. That

morning we were alone together at the creek, I nearly took you then.'

'But you didn't want to believe it would have been the first time.'

'I'm afraid being jealous and being a man go together. I wanted you so badly it was one hell of a nightmare.'

'Agony,' she agreed, and gave a deep sigh. 'You must know I've never lied to you.'

'I did all the time, but I couldn't just accept it without a fight. Then there was Robin. I was angry and shocked. Then when I met you nothing added up. No one so sweet and so tender, so utterly fastidious could have acted as Robin claimed. That girl Danielle, I knew her for what she was, yet clung to her treachery hard.'

'You don't know she was dismissed from the Company,' Rosanne whispered. 'She had a cruel streak, a deliberate knack for causing trouble.'

'The very day I brought you to High Valley I wanted to protect you all my life. I do love you, Rosanne, every least little thing about you. I see how it is with your dancing. You'd still want to go on with it?'

'You'd let me?'

'God!' He groaned and buried his face between her breasts. 'I love you too much. I can't hurt you by denying you your great talent.'

'Hush!' Tenderly she lifted his head. 'My great talent is for loving you.'

'You mean you don't care if you don't go on with your career?' His eyes glittered with an inner agitation. 'After all the years of hard work? Your haunting perfection?'

'Oh, I'll dance!' Her great eyes were filled with life and laughter. 'I'll dance on moonlit nights and there'll be plenty of other times. Our wedding for one.'

'Darling, I don't think I can ask it of you.' He let out a muffled sigh. 'You were a triumph tonight.'

'Was I happy?' She held his face and made him look at her. 'Once the only happiness I had in life was my dancing, but that was before I knew what it was to love, to really love a man. The fiercest necessity in the world—total commitment, body and soul. Besides which, I want children—*our* children. I've always been so alone.'

'Yes, that's important to you.' Ross stared into her brilliant eyes. 'But can you tell me if this is what you're going to want for ever?'

'Can anyone?' She lifted her slender arms and reached for him. 'I love you, Ross. You're what I've been waiting for all my life.'

'Then something had better be done about it,' he said quietly. 'You've had months now to think it over.'

'You mean you did this on purpose?' she asked incredulously.

'You don't understand, darling,' he said gently, 'once you're mine, I'll never let you escape.'

'I don't even want to think about it,' she protested. 'I love you more than anyone and anything in the world. You must know that. You must know I love High Valley. Even from the beginning I had the impression I was coming home.'

'The fact is,' he said tautly, 'I can't go on living there without you.'

Rosanne was seized with a sudden desire to laugh, to cry, to shout her happiness to the sky. 'When can we be married?' she asked.

'The sooner the better,' he said wryly. 'When I make love to you properly for the first time you're going to be Mrs McAdam.'

'Oh, *please*, I want you to love me now.'

'I know.' His hand began to do up the zip on her robe. 'Right now, I'm going to take you out to a late night supper. I want to.'

'So how did you know I was hungry?' She felt beautiful, loved and warm and alive. They were standing together and she put her arms around him, resting her head against his chest. 'Things are going to happen rather quickly now, aren't they?'

'Not quick enough!' He tilted up her face and kissed it. 'I'm going to take care of you all my life.'

Their eyes met and they looked at each other with complete understanding. Out of all the emotional turmoil had come something that was priceless.

She stood on tiptoe and kissed the point of his chin, then she said gaily:

'Come and tell me what you think I should wear!'

What readers say about Harlequin romance fiction...

"I feel as if I am in a different world every time I read a Harlequin."
A.T. * Detroit, Michigan

"Harlequins have been my passport to the world. I have been many places without ever leaving my doorstep."
P.Z. Belvedere, Illinois

"I like Harlequin books because they tell so much about other countries."
N.G., Rouyn, Quebec

"Your books offer a world of knowledge about places and people."
L.J., New Orleans, Louisiana

"Your books turn my...life into something quite exciting."
B.M., Baldwin Park, California

"Harlequins take away the world's troubles and for a while you can live in a world of your own where love reigns supreme."

L.S. * Beltsville. Maryland

"Thank you for bringing romance back to me."

J.W. Tehachapi. California

"I find Harlequins are the only stories on the market that give me a satisfying romance with sufficient depth without being maudlin."

C.S. Bangor Maine

"Harlequins are magic carpets...away from pain and depression...away to other people and other countries one might never know otherwise."

H.R. Akron, Ohio

*Names available on request

Harlequin Romances

The books that let you escape
into the wonderful world of romance!
Trips to exotic places... interesting
plots... meeting memorable people...
the excitement of love.... These are
integral parts of Harlequin Romances —
the heartwarming novels read by
women everywhere.

Many early issues are now available.
Choose from this great selection!

Choose from this list of Harlequin Romance editions.*

*Some of these book were originally published under different titles.

Relive a great love story...
with Harlequin Romances
Complete and mail this coupon today!

Harlequin Reader Service

In U.S.A.
MPO Box 707
Niagara Falls, N.Y. 14302

In Canada
649 Ontario St.
Stratford, Ontario, N5A 6W2

Please send me the following Harlequin Romance novels. I am enclosing my check or money order for $1.25 for each novel ordered, plus 59¢ to cover postage and handling.

☐ 422	☐ 509	☐ 636	☐ 729	☐ 810	☐ 902
☐ 434	☐ 517	☐ 673	☐ 737	☐ 815	☐ 903
☐ 459	☐ 535	☐ 683	☐ 746	☐ 838	☐ 909
☐ 481	☐ 559	☐ 684	☐ 748	☐ 872	☐ 920
☐ 492	☐ 583	☐ 713	☐ 798	☐ 878	☐ 927
☐ 508	☐ 634	☐ 714	☐ 799	☐ 888	☐ 941

Number of novels checked @ $1.25 each = $ _____

N.Y. and Ariz. residents add appropriate sales tax. $ _____

Postage and handling $ _____ .59

         TOTAL $ _____

I enclose _____
(Please send check or money order. We cannot be responsible for cash sent through the mail.)

Prices subject to change without notice.

NAME _____
                (Please Print)

ADDRESS _____

CITY _____

STATE/PROV. _____

ZIP/POSTAL CODE _____

Offer expires June 1, 1981.   01256337141